The Blue Fairy
and other tales of transcendence

Ernest Dempsey

From the World Voices Series

Modern History Press

Library of Congress Cataloging-in-Publication Data

Dempsey, Ernest, 1977-
  The blue fairy and other stories of transcendence / by Ernest
Dempsey.
      p. cm. -- (World voices series ; bk. 1)
  ISBN-13: 978-1-932690-92-7 (trade pbk. : alk. paper)
  ISBN-10: 1-932690-92-1 (trade pbk. : alk. paper)
  I. Title.
  PR9540.9.D46B57 2009
  823'.92--dc22
                              2009011890

For our complete catalog, please visit:
www.ModernHistoryPress.com
info@ModernHistoryPress.com
Tollfree 888-761-6268

Distributed by Ingram Book Group

Modern History Press is an imprint of

Loving Healing Press
5145 Pontiac Trail
Ann Arbor, MI 48105
USA

Dedication

*To the memory of my dear Aunt Farhana,
who left this earth in November 1992*

Contents

Preface

Dear Aunt,

Greetings!

It's Friday, November 17th, 2006, and I have just returned to my hostel room from my cozy office. Fourteen years ago, on the same date, I was a childish teenager, sitting on my bed and playing a solo game with a coin, pen and paper, and a queue of imaginary players. It was Tuesday, November 17th, 1992, when Shais came running to the door of my room, stood at the threshold, and said, "Auntie's dead!" The shock of the news struck me dumb, the coin and pen dropping from my hands. How that day passed is still achingly fresh in my memories. In the form of your eternal departure, death touched my life very closely for the very first time. Within a few days, I fell ill and suffered a one-month illness, the longest of my life.

Death had been but an observation to me before you passed away. People in not-so-near family had died, but it was only on the day of your departure that the phenomenon of death shocked me from within. What had been an observation became an experience. How could someone so loving, so kind, so beautiful and lively, so close to our hearts, suddenly perish forever? I could not believe the news that a grown-up, 33-year-old woman could die in childbirth while the little life that had not yet opened its eyes to the world still lived. But such is our existence here. We humans are as much given to evil chances as any other animals or living forms on this planet.

Surviving your death was the hardest experience. A kind of unbearable emptiness filled us. We had to accept it and we simply couldn't. The whole family snuggled together for over a month and kept the spirit of belongingness alive. You were the spirit then. Six months after your death, the horrible news of the death of our uncle, your youngest brother, made death a Sword of Damocles on our peace. Death became stark reality and scared us to the core of our being. Things kept getting worse after that and the unity of the family weakened every passing day. Today we have in our family history several deaths, including the painful suicide of your teenage son Sheroz.

Personally, I suffered the worst by your death. Time did its job of anointing the wounds. Today I am 30 years of age, with a job, and you know what? My passion for writing has finally earned me the publication of a book. I remember you once called me "a philosopher" when I gave some answer that was overly serious for my age at that time. And now the imprint of that word is assuming fresh colors as my thinking grows deeper, though still not deep enough to touch that love you held for us all.

As my second book is being planned for publication, I have thought of making it special with reference to you. The book is about death, and to whom else but you would I dedicate this publication? I have sketched a brief glimpse of my memories of you as seen through my eyes in moments of deep inspiration and affection. As I walk along the road of passion toward the destination of success with the written word, your love serves as my inexhaustible light. It has lit my way before and it will keep my spirits glowing.

I have a metaphor for your presence in my life. It's called The Blue Fairy: blue for the limitless sky, which is your abode, and fairy for your kindness and affection that few others have been able to offer us.

Always your loving nephew,
Ernest

Ally Wells' Birthday Secret

No woman on campus was as lively and beautiful as the 20-year-old Ally Wells. Given her soothing countenance and cherubic smile, both faculty and fellow students had universally adored her since the day she had stepped into the department of performing arts. Still, there was something aloof about her: the fact that she never invited anyone to recognize her birthday, nor allowed anyone to arrange a gift celebration for her on or off the campus. Just a couple of days before October 18th, her birthday, she would mysteriously disappear and return on the 20th or shortly thereafter.

A number of assumptions went around among those who knew and admired her (and who didn't?): she was a miser; she wanted to arouse curiosity; she had a secret affair; she was a psycho; and so on. Ally never confirmed any of these and she always dealt with questions with "Sorry, no explanation." The secret of her birthday celebration robbed many of their sleep for three years before it was finally discovered by none other than me.

It happened on October 19th, last year, when I was returning to my dormitory by bus after a brief visit to my home. At the next stop after I got on, I saw the pretty figure of Ally Wells dressed in black entering the bus. She looked adorable, as always. Seeing me and a neighboring vacant seat, Ally smiled and sat by my side. We exchanged greetings and I immediately remembered that the day before had been her birthday.

"Ally, can I ask you something?" I could not resist thinking about her birthday mystery.

"Yes, I think you're curious to know if my presence here has any connection with my birthday secret." She was so intelligent as well.

"Tell me, if you don't mind," said I, feeling the coming of a grand secret. "I promise I won't breathe it out."

"Okay," she said, and with a bright face and steady voice, started to narrate. "October 18th is a special day for me. You know why, because it's my birthday, but more so because it's a day when

I was honored in the most special way I have ever known. Every year I disappear to celebrate my birthday not with friends or family, or a boyfriend, but with someone who died for me."

Her last words came to me as a shock.

"Who was that person?" I could not harness my dismay, my mind spinning faster than an electron.

"My uncle Kevin," she answered peacefully, a deep look of respect and affection shining in her eyes.

"Your uncle!" I could not help exclaiming.

"That's right. My uncle Kevin, as my mom and dad tell me, was a lonesome young man of 28 when I was born. Being the first child in my generation of the Wells family, I was coddled by all. Uncle Kevin worked as an editor in Roseville, from where I got on this bus just now. He remained very busy with his work, never got married, and rarely visited his parents and brothers. But he always called home and asked about me. Only later, I came to know he had been coping with the fear that some accident might engulf me. When I was going to be one year old, Uncle Kevin cried with joy. He bought several gifts, put off all his engagements, and arranged to attend my first birthday.

Then something happened which no one could have anticipated. A horrible highway accident claimed the lives of seven people on the bus, including Uncle Kevin. Gifts he had sent ahead reached us the very next day after the accident. Since he can't come to see me on my birthday, I visit his resting place every year on this special day with gifts and flowers to let him see how well I'm doing and how badly I miss him. That's the secret of my birthday. And I don't mind if you share it with everyone."

"How long have you been celebrating your birthday this way?" I asked, nearly mesmerized by her account.

"Ever since I turned sixteen and got the courage to travel alone, I've been visiting Uncle Kevin by myself," she answered. "Before that, we lived in Roseville, where my parents accompanied me to his resting place."

"Ally, just asking, if you will allow," I started, and seeing her nod in her distinctive, cute manner, proceeded, "haven't you ever feared that traveling thus might prove dangerous for you? If I were in your place, I would think twice before boarding a bus on October 18th." Ally laughed gently at this.

"I'm not superstitious," she said, lightly. "But it did occur to me that some accident might take my life. Then it soothed me to think that such an event wouldn't really take me away from my loved ones, just as it didn't take Uncle Kevin away from us. In fact, I think, I'd be closer to my uncle then, wouldn't I?"

The beauty of Ally's question kept me entranced through the rest of our travel together. Ally Wells remained as beautiful for us as ever. She made my feelings about life and love more beautiful by sharing her birthday secret with me. So now I generously share her secret with everyone.

An Innocent Crime

Steve Connors stopped at the library gate and bent his head to the left whence the voice had called. He saw a slender young girl, conservatively dressed, approaching him. Her face seemed familiar, but Steve couldn't recollect where he had seen her. He waited patiently while she came slowly toward him. It appeared from her gait that she was either ill or very weak. She said "Hello" as she got close, and Steve saw that her face was pale, very pale indeed, under curly black hair, a lock of which hung along her narrow forehead.

"Hello!" Steve replied, looking at her face, trying to recognize her. She read the uncertainty in his eyes and asked, "You are Mr. Steve Connors. Am I right?"

"Yes, do I know you?" he asked, still trying to recollect what was so familiar in her face.

"I'm Martha... Martha Dorey." She gave faint smile, saying, "Can I talk to you somewhere alone, please?" Steve shrugged in uncertainty.

"Well, perhaps we can sit inside," he said, taking a step in through the entrance. She thanked him with a cough and walked beside him. They chose a table downstairs were they might be alone. She sat opposite him and he saw that her face betrayed repressed pain as she breathed in. She looked down at the table quietly for a minute, as if trying to consider how to start saying something, while he looked at her expectantly. It was a little bothersome to sit with someone so apparently familiar, yet fail to remember exactly who she was. And the way she could call out his name while also recognizing him from a distance! She definitely knew him.

Suddenly she lifted her eyes to his face and said, "My name is Martha Dorey."

"Yes, you told me at the gate," he replied with a slight nod.

"Oh!" She smiled listlessly. "Uh...you don't seem to remember me."

"I'm afraid not," he said mildly, with a formal smile.

"I used to work at Mrs. Anne Geoffrey's, your neighbor's," she said.

"Oh, indeed!" He remembered suddenly. "You're the sister of Kim, the girl who worked for my mother, aren't you?"

"That's right," she confirmed. "I'm Kim's sister." She broke into a cough, and when she lifted her eyes to him again, he saw the redness in them.

"It's nice to see you again after that long a time," he said with a kind smile, continuing to look at her. "I mean, it's been some fourteen years or so since I last saw you. You used to come with Kim."

She breathed out brief, diseased laughter and said, "Yes, that was fifteen years ago. You were just a boy then."

"Oh, yes," he laughed. "And you just a thoughtful little lady who never spoke a word until asked, right?"

A veil of sorrow covered her face as she looked from his face to the shelves beyond; perhaps she missed her past. He felt somewhat uneasy at her expression.

"Are you all right?" he asked with solicitude.

"Yes." She stressed the word and, looking back at him with humility, said, "I wanted to talk to you about something."

"Well, sure," he encouraged her. "But just tell me. How did you find me?"

"I work for Mrs. Wayne at Heamesville. Her brother, Karl, told me about you," she answered.

"Oh, yes, Karl's my colleague. He's a good guy… But where is your family now? I mean Kim, your mother, and that roguish cousin of yours, what was his name?" He narrowed his eyes, trying to recollect the name.

"Edgar. He's Kim's husband now. They got married soon after mother died, five years ago," she said glumly.

"I'm sorry!"

"It's all right." She locked the fingers of her hands together, saying, "I went to your office an hour ago. They told me I could find you here."

"Well, thank you, Martha. I'm pleasantly surprised to see you here, but you really don't look in good health. May I ask what the matter is?"

She grew still at this question, her eyes fixed on the shelf behind him, and she looked lost in an undefined space. Then he saw tears welling up in her somber hazel eyes. She pressed her lips inward against each other. Then, with an effort, she sighed and said, "I'm... I'm about to die... perhaps." And with this she quickly repressed a sob.

Her words stunned him. He looked at her with still eyes. Her face, for a moment, looked white as death itself.

"Uh... it's... it's really a bad thing to hear," he started, trying to find something reasonable to say. "I'm really sorry. May I ask why, if it doesn't offend you?"

She glanced at him, and for a moment fixed on the shelf again. Then she gathered her strength and said, "The doctor told me that my tissues, mainly of my heart, have deadened. I'm going to be operated on next week. I may fall into a coma, in which case I'd be given euthanasia." She stopped to breathe before going on to say, "I've already signed the papers."

Steve kept his gaze on her face. He didn't know how to express his sympathy toward her. And before he could come up with something worth saying, she preceded him.

"I have something important to say to you. Actually, I have something that belongs to you, and you must keep it."

Steve frowned a bit in wonder. "What could that be?" he asked.

She put her hand in her black purse and took out something wrapped in a brown cloth. She then took the cloth off and extended her arm to him. He saw a wristwatch in her pale fingers. The watchband was red. She was looking down at the table, waiting for him to take the watch.

"What is it?" he asked with some wonder.

"It's your watch," she said, looking at him. "Your uncle, Mr. Smith, brought you this. Do you remember?"

He remembered suddenly. "On Christmas, back in '79!" Then he took it and turned it in his fingers a couple of times. "How did you get it? Did I drop it somewhere?" He was still lost in wonder.

She looked down. "No." She hesitated a little and then uttered meekly, "I stole it from you."

The awkwardness of the situation struck him head on. A dying girl was there to return to him the watch she had stolen in their childhood: an innocent crime for which she sought penance in the shadow of death.

He didn't know what to say. He kept looking at the watch in sorrow and inexplicable guilt.

Then she looked at him with light clear eyes, her gaze piercing through him.

"I liked it a lot when you wore it. We were poor, and I craved it from the first day I saw it on your wrist. I'd dream about it every night. And one day when I found the chance to be alone in your room, I took it secretly. You thought it was lost and you seemed to care rather little about it. But I haven't been happy all these years while living under the dismal thought of unfair possession." She stopped to breathe.

Steve remained silent, almost dumb. Then her voice moved into him.

"I used to wear it, secretly, at night. In the day I kept it hidden under my bed. I tried to return it to you a couple of times but my heart failed me. So I kept it, believing that someday I'd be able to return it. I think now it's time. You would forgive me for this?" She looked at him in entreaty.

"Oh yes, of course!" He really felt awkward. "It was an innocent crime, just like laughter or something." He sounded silly to his own ears. "You need not have taken the pains."

Tears rushed to her eyes. He looked down.

"I hope you get well," he said, changing the topic. "Don't despair, your operation may result in a new life."

Her gaze shifted from the shelf to his face and returned to its previous point. Then she moved a little forward in her seat and said, "I think I should go now."

He shrugged and said, "If there's anything I can do for you, I'd be happy to."

"No, thank you!" She stood up. "I feel better. I'll inform you if I live." The stress on "if" was desperate and held a yearning, a staggering desire to live.

"I wish you well." He stood up too.

"Thank you!" She looked at his face for one last time and went off. He turned to see her leave, hearing only the rustling of her skirt.

As she went out the door, he glanced at the watch in his hand. It showed 5:30. A dullness filled with sorrow overtook him. Very slowly, he went to where she had been a moment before. He sat in the chair she had sat in, the watch in his hand. His glance wandered to the shelf where she had been looking while talking to him. The reflection of the light coming from the window had turned the glass of the shelf into a mirror. He could see his face in it. And it told him how he appeared.

Cry of Pain

Another light pricking sensation shot through Stephen's back. He uttered a faint, brief moan. It was the third day since he had first acquired that skin condition. First, a rash appeared on his back, his chest, and a little below his armpit. He took it for the effect of heat, as the summer was brutally hot that year. But that morning, one of his friends told him that it was herpes zoster, a viral attack. He decided to see the doctor the next morning after his fever was over. He figured he could bear the pain for just one night.

As bedtime approached, he thought he should have seen a doctor earlier. The rash had grown into small blisters filled with a viscous whitish fluid. Those on his back pricked him every few minutes. He picked up a draft of his graduation thesis and began to review it. The pain seemed to intensify a little. It was hard to concentrate on reading, so he gave up, deciding to review it again in the morning. He went to the bathroom to wash. The first thing he thought of, on reentering his room, was to take up his "Halliwell's Guide to Movies." *Perhaps it would be a good way to kill time*, he thought.

At this moment there was a knock on the door. His friend Jerry came in. They exchanged hellos.

"You've been out all day?" Stephen asked.

"Yes. We were out. Andy is dead," Jerry said in a sinking tone.

Stephen could hardly hear what he said, his face and attention directed toward the cupboard.

"What? You went to bring Andy here?" he inquired.

"Andy is dead." Jerry stressed each word.

"Oh, God! No!" Stephen was shocked. "When?" He felt his heart sinking. Pain had gone for the moment.

"This morning."

"But, how did he die?" Stephen felt tears struggling to surface from inside him.

"He was killed by his brother." Jerry went on to explain how a bitter argument between Andy and his younger brother had led to the tragic event.

Grief spread its wings over Stephen. Tears started from his eyes.

"I think you'd better wash your face. We may go out to have some coffee. You need it, and I do, too." Jerry's words sounded reasonable.

Stephen obeyed listlessly. As he was returning from the bathroom, his pain woke up again.

Over the next hour, they shared their memories of Andy. Stephen returned to his room with pain increasing every second. Even reading was impossible. Needles went on pricking his back, causing his breathing to become unsteady now and then.

Then his amiable friend Fred came to stay with him for the night. Stephen knew that Jerry would have told Fred about his illness. Fred's arrival relieved him for a while. They sat up till midnight.

The pain suddenly became severe. Stephen began to moan, his thoughts arrested by Andy's murder. He felt as if Andy's wounds were mutilating his body. Fred suggested taking him to the hospital, but Stephen refused to go, saying he would endure it all. The pricks had now become little electric shocks, each jolting his back. He looked at the clock. It was past 1:00 a.m., a long time until dawn. How was he supposed to bear it?

Stephen told Fred to go to sleep and switched off the lights. Shocks continued to shoot through him. He was trying to stop moaning, for he did not want to make Fred rise again and try to console him. The painkillers did not seem to bring any relief either. About half an hour passed like that.

Suddenly Stephen rose again in his bed with a sob. Fred turned on his other side.

"Fred!" Stephen called. "I need to turn on the light!" Fred did it for him.

"This is not going to end," Stephen said in near soliloquy.

"What?" Fred did not know what he meant. "You mean the pain?"

"The pain, and the fear, and lies, cruel things, all very...." He was delirious.

Fred did not understand. He watched Stephen uttering in his confusion. The shocks now came in pairs, each pair rhythmically succeeding the first. Stephen looked at the clock. It was half past two. Time was so slow. *Why did it not run?* Morning was still a far cry. Fred insisted on taking him to the hospital or calling an ambulance. But he was doggedly refusing, showing irritation with pain.

"Morning!" he cried. "When is it going to come? I am so tired. I can't bear it anymore." Fred hugged him.

Suddenly Stephen seemed to feel revulsion. "Give me a pen and paper," he demanded of Fred.

"Look..." Fred tried to reason with him.

"No!" Stephen cried. "Give me a pen and paper! Give them to me now!" Fred obeyed. Stephen sat leaning on the paper, and started to write: "This is my body. It can be tortured, can be wounded, but it cannot be taken from me." He threw down the pen, held the paper close, and sternly examined it. Then he crumpled it in his hand and threw it away.

His eyes wandered back to the clock. Time was slow, almost still. He felt Time's treachery. It was despotic, thriving on his helplessness. He could not bring the morning, the light, the people, and the birds. Everything was against him in that instant. Needles pricked his back. But he did not feel the excruciating pain as he did a while ago. He never remembered when he dropped off. What he did remember were his words, written at the end of his soliloquy:

> Wounded is my body
> Bleeding is my heart
> Pierced is my soul
> I am all a cry of pain

* * *

It was more than four months later in his hometown that Stephen was going to see his aunt who had returned from Europe to visit her native land again after three years absence. As he walked toward her house, a sharp sense of unease possessed him.

He knew it could be a painful visit because his cousin, the eldest son of the aunt he was going to see, had died in Copenhagen. His aunt had not yet been informed, but she was going to know that evening or the next morning.

As usual, she received Stephen in jolly spirits, hugging him and kissing him on his forehead. They sat to talk. He was trying to invite calm with his manner. Her motherly instincts were defying his effort.

"I am a little worried for my children," she said. "None of them has called for three days. I wonder why. Rob usually calls daily."

"They're too busy, I suppose," he said, struggling to stifle his frailty. "You need not worry."

"Well... I am especially worried about Ricky." Her words made Stephen's heart stop for a second. Ricky was dead.

"Why about him?" he fought to ask.

"He's been working very hard these days, not taking a bit of rest. He might fall ill." There was a concern in her tone that was reaching Stephen's heart.

"Tell me about Ricky." He led himself along another way of escape, one he felt would do for a while. "Ricky's been there 18 years. I've nearly forgotten his face. How does he look?"

She smiled. Her face was adorned with maternal affection, sweet and welcoming. He felt the warmth of it, and it pierced him with its tenderness.

"He is tall, strong, very handsome," she said with pride. "He works so hard. Sometimes I argue with him, begging him not to exhaust himself, but he is mad for success."

It was hard for Stephen to keep his countenance. His endurance was wavering and his hand clasped the arm of the chair. No grieved look was permissible for the moment. He led the topic another way. After half an hour, she received a couple of visitors and he was ready to leave.

She hugged him, and spoke words of prayer. The motherly touch of her arms anointed the smoldering angst in his heart. Before exiting, he cast a final glance at her. She was watching him with a kind smile. He fought to hide the wounds of his own.

That night, while he was alone in his room, reading a book with an absent mind, he thought of the calamity that was impending on his family. He could not stop thinking about tomorrow when all of them, including his mother, would be mourning Ricky's death. His aunt, who had returned to her hometown to make preparations for her youngest son's wedding, would see her eldest one's corpse. The corpse of his cousin was to arrive the next day. It was nearly midnight. Time was running fast.

Suddenly he had an intense desire to stop time. He looked at the clock. It was ticking recklessly. He knew it would not stop. Time knows no tears. Clocks have no eyes, no brain, no heart, nothing. Helplessness brought tears into his eyes. He knew he could not stop time. He lay immovable on the bed. The clock ticked steadily.

Dimmer

Andy didn't like the way Dave took up the topic. "Don't waste a single day," Dave stressed. "I'm also having doubts about my sight. We'll pay the City Hospital a visit. Agreed?"

"Yeah, maybe some other day." Andy tried to mask the platitude with a grin.

But that other day was soon part of his experience. It was crowded as they sat in the waiting room, full of patients, each one showing a distinct face, but all wearing looks of misery and anguished patience.

They waited for about an hour, utterly bored. Just as Andy was to enter the physician's examination room for his turn, an elderly, weak, feverish lady grabbed the handle, looking into his eyes with an irresistible appeal to pity. Andy shrugged, pouted, and went straight out of the waiting room, followed by Dave, who cried, "What the hell do you think you're doing?"

This was discussed for a long time the following day, over coffee. Andy's friends Kyle and Alvin made him read, or try to read, almost every printed word in their surroundings. They wanted to see if he really was nearsighted. Andy was fed up.

"You'll need to watch all your favorite flicks again, buddy, after you get your glasses," Smith kidded.

"It's no more than another of his contrived apprehensions." Kyle was unbearably frank.

Andy looked at them. They all looked like suckers. He stood up with a startle.

Kyle turned serious. "Let me take you to my Uncle Sean, you know him. He'll help you see clearer." Andy nodded and left.

Back at the office, he was told that his request for a transfer had been turned down.

"We really need you here, Andy. Wait for a few months, and I assure you that we'll send you anywhere you want. Just let us get out of the shit here." This was Mr. Sinclair, his manager and a first-class asshole. Andy could never come to terms with the fact that such a rotten figure held authority over him. Life seemed absurd at such moments.

He spent four busy hours at his office before puking up his only snack of the day. Mr. Sinclair let him go with a frown, and Andy rushed out as if fearing asphyxiation. He waited for the bus, forcing breath into his lungs. A stuffy and populous city lay before him, the vision of it clouded by his weakened sight.

He used to keep his vision confined to things close to him. There was no need to fix his gaze on faraway objects. But still, he couldn't resist Kyle's insistence on a check-up. So he went to Kyle's plump, sleepy Uncle Sean, who suggested a pair of minus-one spectacles. They fetched a pair, and as Andy put them on, he grew excited about his new vision.

"How's that?" he was prompted.

"Clear, but it seems the world's grown smaller." He was peering around.

"That's normal. You'll adjust soon."

"Yeah, I hope so." Andy removed the glasses.

Angela arrived at 9:00. She was tired but happy to see him with glasses on.

"Congratulations! You've got four now," she said, laughing.

"You look like a little doll." He took them off. She hugged him.

"What about Stanley's case?" Andy asked at the dinner table. Angela looked serious, now, serious and despondent. She sighed.

"He'll get off," she answered faintly.

"What!" Andy drew back. She only blinked.

"And in cold blood! How come?" His voice was replete with protest.

"They say it was an accident and not an intentional murder."

"What the hell do they mean by intention?" He stood up, raising his voice.

"Andy, please! I know he was a dear friend of yours, but..."

"But it doesn't matter, because the evidence that this was a murder is weak and it proves that it was an accident. So it wasn't a murder in cold blood! I wonder how blood can ever be cold?" She didn't answer.

"Why don't you argue the prejudiced intolerance that caused Stanley's murder at the hands of a fanatic?" He grimaced and reddened.

"We've claimed it. It's no use. The court won't consider it. If there had been even a five-percent chance, I'd still have…"

"This is very important. Well, this is the most important…"

"Andy, please!" Angela felt sick. "I didn't make the rules." He looked at her for a minute and then went out, stamping off to his bedroom.

Kyle expressed his sorrow at this. "What if he's given a death sentence now? Stanley isn't coming back."

"At least we'll see things more clearly and distinctly," Andy returned, placidly now.

"The question is, do we want to?" Kyle asked.

"Then, why these glasses?" He took them off and tossed them onto the table. Kyle looked into his eyes; they were as clear as ever.

"I wonder whether you really need them."

"Well, I've got to go now." Andy stood up and so did Kyle.

After saying goodbye to Kyle at the *Fantasy Ware*, Andy got himself a cab. It traversed the flow of vehicles and people on the road. He looked out the window, now wearing glasses again. Everything looked clear. A demonstration was on way at the Senate building. Dressed in white, members of *The Irenic* were protesting against the approved construction of a kickboxing club in the *Amusement Area*. A band of singers was dancing along, singing "City of Peace." Their faces were lit with hope and confidence. They all had spirit, the spirit of change. And all that looked so clear in the stuffy afternoon.

So Andy took off his glasses and put them back in his coat. From an inside pocket, he took out his sunglasses and put them on. Things grew dimmer beyond their dense screen. He kept looking out the window. As the taxi moved on, "City of Peace" grew fainter and fainter. He was carried away in the cab, looking out the window through his dark glasses.

Just a Kilometer

Gary Walters slowly rose to his feet. He knew he was not yet past danger. Being shot, he had pretended to be dead while the robbers sacked the store. Fifteen minutes before, all three of his fellow workers had been shot dead, one in the head, one in the neck, and the other twice in the chest. Gary received a bullet in his thigh.

He lay still until they ran off. His wound had bled a great deal, though he had been pressing it with his palm even while he lay motionless on the ground. He took a few steps to get out of the store. The nearest point where he could expect some help was the village post office, about a kilometer south. The desolate path confirmed that he had to rely on himself for making it to the post office. Pain had already started its war on him.

Weakness of body and spirit seized his steps. For a moment, darkness covered his sight and he felt like falling dead for real.

"Clara!" The thought of his wife had made him speak her name in a faltering tone. Her face rose up before his eyes, smiling softly at him. He took another step. A pang shot through him. He saw his hand, covered with his blood, pressing his thigh. *"Death!"* The word rang in his head, calling again the darkness that the thought of Clara had dispelled.

"No!" he sobbed, taking another step.

"Clara!" he called again. Her face came back to him. This time, he could see her neck, her bosom, her hands working the knitting needles. He remembered that this morning she had told him she was making another sweater for him. *Would I live now to see that*, he thought. With his wound, a kilometer seemed impossibly far. Clara's face hovered before his eyes. Her hands kept knitting. A cool breeze blew upon his face. A modicum of relief poured a little strength into him. Her smooth, shapely fingers played cleverly with wool and needles. Pain lost its intensity for a moment. He smiled faintly.

"Clara!" Her name brought her face closer to him. She was smiling at him, her hands complacently knitting an immaculate white garment. He thought of the sweater she was knitting. His step gained some confidence. Pain thwarted him.

But he could carry on. Clara was there, smiling, knitting for him. A kilometer was not that long to go. He had covered some part of it. He knew he could carry on without collapsing.

Mother Mary

A sharp cry from the baby pierced the still air.

"Do something, Mary!" The grandmother rocks the writhing mass in her lap. Mary is pale, looking at her child stealthily for want of courage.

"The ambulance will be on its way," she mutters, biting her lip. The baby's nostrils are flaring; her lips are purple, turning black.

"The drip, Mary," says the grandmother. "Take heart! You're a doctor!"

"I can't," she denies. The baby's breath makes a whistle. Mary is shaken from within. She rushes inside, takes the drip, and comes to the infant.

"Hold her," she instructs in desperate confidence, and inserts the needle into a vein, the baby's head now dangling as if near death. The fluid flows into it. She steps back and starts dithering about in her unease. The baby's face is darkening.

Mary goes to the front door and peers outside. There is no trace of the ambulance. She returns and resumes her anxious ramble, glancing every few moments at the dying thing.

"Will she live?" asks the grandmother, in disbelief.

"I pray she will, but..." Mary cannot speak further. Then there is the emergency siren of the ambulance. They take the baby and rush outside. The empty house looks their way.

The ambulance returns before long. With a mourning cry, the elderly woman enters the house. Mary is pale with eyes strained and tearless. She walks in a trance, not looking at the swaddled and dead baby carried by the wailing older woman.

"Cover her," Mary utters with effort. "Don't show her to me." The woman's cries grow louder. Neighbors begin coming to share the grief. Mary is silent, lost somewhere in unbound darkness. Time passes without her having any sense of it.

The baby's father comes in, sees her little face, kisses her cheek, and sits beside his wife. She does not look at him. She knows she will not see anyone or anything. Her eyes are open but blind. Caretakers are now serving coffee to the guests. A priest enters with some neighbor men and relatives. The baby is to be taken for burial. Mary looks away.

They are bringing her for a last look. She closes her eyes and touches the still, soft cheeks.

"Won't you look at her?" asks her husband. She shakes her head, with lips and eyes as if sewn shut. They have taken the baby out, but Mary's eyes are still closed, and she keeps on shaking her head. Someone is hugging her.

"She's gone, Mary," she hears. "Pray for her. She's gone to heaven."

* * *

The days are now sorrowful, and the nights are still more grief-filled. Mary speaks little, eats little, and hardly responds to her husband. She hears Jenny's infant son, when he cries, in the adjacent house. His cries are so very like those of her own Bette. When Mary is half asleep in the easy chair, basking in the sunny yard, his cries shake her up. She starts to rush to her Bette. The next moment she remembers it is only Jason. It dejects the mother in her. Her Bette is gone. She cannot rush to someone else's child. People will think her crazy. Sometimes she wishes all the children were dead. Grief would take over, but then there would be no more afterwards. There would be no child, and no mother to mourn again.

Bette's belongings are all locked up in a closet, its key kept by the grandmother. Mary thinks of giving all the things to Jason. Envy checks her. These were all Bette's. No one deserves them. No one can have them. Jason's cries still rend her heart.

"Is Jenny's baby ill?" Mary asks her mother-in-law. She says that he is. Mary has a bad feeling and then a wicked one: *Illness is taking others' children, too; my Bette wasn't the only victim.*

Another day passes and Jason's cries do not cease. Mary listens anxiously, walking near the wall that joins the houses. The cries grow louder and nearer. Mary's heart is sinking. *What is happening to the baby?* she thinks.

The cries come to their house door. She rushes to open it. Jenny is standing there, pale with fear and apprehension, holding her baby in its woolen blanket.

"Daniel has dropped the telephone," Jenny says. "We need to call the emergency service. Jason is not well."

"Give him to me," Mary takes the child and examines him. A high fever! Her mother-in-law is not home.

"Hold him." She gives Jenny the baby and rushes to the closet. It's locked and there's no time to find the key. Fetching the hammer, she strikes the lock hard and breaks it after three desperate blows. Leaning inside the closet, she pulls everything out: injections, drip, syringes, toys, everything. Jenny is crying in worry and helplessness. Mary flashes out of the room.

"Hold him this way," she orders the mother, and pushes the needle into the baby's hip. He shrieks. Jenny sobs. Mary throws away the syringe and takes the baby in her lap.

"There, there," she says, rocking the child in her lap.

"Go and call the hospital, quick!" she commands Jenny, while rubbing Jason's wee face with a wet towel. Jenny returns in seconds.

"They'll be here," she says, looking at the child.

"Will he live?" Jenny looks at Mary with questioning eyes.

"Yes, he will." Mary is rocking him gently, feeling the heat of his little body on her fingers. The baby is nearly pacified. Jenny's sobs are fading. The ambulance arrives. Mary carries the baby. The house looks their way.

Within an hour, they are back. Jason is better. He is asleep. Mary rambles about in the yard. She remembers Bette's toys, things she never had a chance to play with. She takes them to Jenny in the evening.

"You saved him," says Jenny in obligation.

"I told you he would live." Mary smiles and kisses the little sleeping soul.

Mary sleeps well that night. Jason's cries are over and Mary has a sweet dream. Bette is smiling at her, stretching her wee, tender arms toward her, loving her from heaven.

Oblivion

Jill put a rose on Edwin's grave because no one else would. She thought little about Edwin on her way back home, lest she lose her way. At ten years old, she was quite oblivious to many such things.

Betty and Sam stood still upon seeing her. "Is Dad inside?" she asked them.

"Yes," replied Sam, staring at her. Jill went straight inside. Her father was there, in the kitchen.

"Where have you been?" He gazed at her with a frown.

"At the cemetery." She glanced away, her voice steady.

"You stubborn girl! I told you not to go there." Jill looked at him. He was fierce. She trembled, turned back, and ran out. She could hear her father behind, yelling at her. "Jill, stop! I'm telling you, if I ever..."

At the school, Jill didn't sit in class; she used to forget lessons and get scolded for it. She stayed beyond the fence, hiding behind the walnut tree, watching the boys and girls play on the green grass. Rain came and changed the scene. They all ran inside, closing the doors and windows. Jill stayed there, as still as if she had forgotten to leave.

Raindrops trickled down her golden brown hair and she looked at the ground in a trance. Voices, laughter, and cries of excitement faded slowly, but they were there, still there; she felt them, oblivious to the rain and cold.

At supper, she refrained from looking at her father. She finished earlier than everyone else and went to her bed without saying a word or hearing one. Edwin's photo was inside her pillowcase. She took it from beneath her head and gazed at it. He was smiling in his uniform, holding a gun in his hands. It was the very thing that had ended his life.

She heard footfalls outside her door. Quickly placing the photo inside the pillowcase, she closed her eyes. The door was pushed open meekly. *It's Betty for sure*, she thought, lying still.

"Jill," Betty called faintly. Jill opened her eyes. Betty must have wanted to ask her something, so Jill sat up in bed.

"Yes?" She looked at Betty, who seemed a mixture of thoughtful, sleepy, and confused.

"What does traitor mean?" Betty asked.

Jill was cold.

"Have you been asking Sam?"

"Yes, but it seems he doesn't know, and Dad won't tell me."

Jill got out of bed and went to her. "People say a person who abandons faith is a traitor." She was looking into her sister's eyes.

"Faith?" Betty frowned.

"Trust, Betty, I think it means trust." She herself was uncertain. A haze of thoughts clouded her head.

"Jill, you don't know either!" Betty turned back in disappointment. "Who am I supposed to ask?" She went out and Jill could hear her say, "Miss Neve says words I can never understand."

It was times like these when Jill was afraid of Betty. Her little innocent questions were like open wounds. She felt the pain, but she couldn't touch.

The next day, there was a thunderstorm in the early morning. Jill was happy at first. It was pleasing to work in the warm kitchen, giving Dad a hand in making breakfast, with rain showering outside. But as she thought of Edwin's grave, a hidden albatross held her. She must cover the grave with something, a plastic tarp perhaps, but it wasn't possible.

There were heavy showers outside and Dad was home. She watched Dad. He was calm and nonchalant. Obviously he wasn't going out to work today; no one would come for riding lessons in the rain.

As she grew sure of his presence at home throughout the day, her heart sank within her. Sam and Betty were sent to tidy their room, and Jill started to cut the vegetables. Dad was cleaning his rifle and oiling it. She worked quietly, peeking at the clock and then at Dad from time to time. At 10:25, when Dad was repairing the closet, Brady, the farm's watchman, called out for him. Brady sounded worried. As Dad went out to see him, Jill became all ears, in hope of hearing Dad say, "Okay, I'm coming with you."

This didn't happen. Dad came in again.

"Is everything all right?" Jill asked.

"Well, Timmy has hurt his leg playing soccer, and I need to go with Brady for half an hour. Don't leave the house till I get back, all right?"

Jill's heart was strained. It leaped at first on hearing that he was to leave, but half an hour was too short a time for her to both cover Edwin's grave and return unnoticed. Dad took his mackintosh and went out.

She stood silently, confused about what to do. Then she rushed to the store down the road to find a tarp for covering the grave. She decided to feign something like hearing a cry outside, but she had to go, no matter how heavy the rain or how muddy the path might be. There was nothing suitable in the store.

She went back home and went to the basement, trying to remember where she had once put an old plastic sheet. Looking behind the boxes and under the junk piles, she couldn't find it. Her heart started stewing. "The stable, yes it must be there," she said to herself, and ran across the intervening lawn to get there.

But she was stymied again. Father was expected back soon, and Sam and Betty would be looking for her to help them. It was raining heavily outside, and she had forgotten where she had last seen that tarp. She grew tired, returned to the kitchen, and sat on the stool, looking exhaustedly at the pieces of shredded carrot scattered about the table.

Sam came down and saw her. "Have you been to Edwin's grave?" he asked.

"No," she replied softly. "Why?"

Sam didn't say anything. He just stared at her. Jill felt awkward, feeling as if Sam knew what she had been looking for.

"Edwin's grave is fairly sheltered. The tree cover there is quite thick. I don't think we need to cover it, or do we?" The words came spontaneously from her lips.

Sam shook his head indifferently and said," I'm going to do my homework. Will you help me?""

"Yes, let's go!" And they went up the stairs, both of them keeping silent.

Miss Cohen was happy to see Jill in class after a whole week. Noticing her solitude, she called her to the office. She was alone there.

"I'm sorry about your brother, Jill." She was very polite. Jill had always liked her.

"Thank you, Miss Cohen." Jill looked down.

"Do feel confident to ask me if there is anything I can do for you."

"Yes." She remained silent for a while, and then looked at her teacher.

"People hate Edwin. They say he was a traitor. Is that right?"

"Oh, Jill! What do you think?" Miss Cohen was as affectionate as ever.

Jill kept silent. After a minute she looked up. "I don't know." She felt like crying.

"Then tell me, what do you want to know, whether your brother was a traitor or whether it's right to hate a traitor after death?" Miss Cohen asked.

Jill watched her face with teary eyes, saying nothing, as if trying to select the right question. It was another one of her trials, but Miss Cohen wouldn't let it loom any longer.

"Whether Edwin was a traitor or not means something different to different people. He might have been a bad man in the eyes of others, but not in yours or mine, and I am sure that you are as certain of his fairness as I am. And to whether we should hate someone after his death or not, I say no. We can love someone after his death, but we shouldn't hate him. Beyond our world is no place for fear, anger, or hatred. I suppose love is the most decent and perhaps the only gift we can offer the dead. Isn't it, honey?"

And Jill burst into tears. Miss Cohen hugged her. And Jill was all tears in her arms.

Dad was arguing with some neighbors beside the stable. Jill went straight into the house. Mrs. Canes had come to wash the clothing, so Jill started to give her a hand.

Dad came in after half an hour, his face shedding its irritation and sadness. As he exchanged a brief look with them both, Mrs. Canes seemed to hide something, something she would have talked about had Jill not been there. Dad went into his office and Jill sank into her thoughts.

Young, jolly Edwin had joined the army according to his father's will. When they heard about him selling national secrets to an enemy state, they were all shocked. He was then sent to a disputed tract along a creek. From there his mutilated body was retrieved, shot to pieces. His coffin didn't bear the national flag and his body wasn't cleaned or prepared for viewing. They just thrust him underground, without even a headstone.

But no one knew that Jill had secretly prepared a wooden marker for Edwin's grave. It lay there beneath the toys in her toy box. She intended to fix it by the grave in the evening.

Betty was running a temperature and Sam sat with her on the bed, reading to her from her favorite storybook.

"You are going to be fine." Jill caressed her sister's hot cheek. Betty paid no attention to Jill because she was absorbed in the story that Sam continued to read.

Jill went out and heard Dad saying, "They can bury him elsewhere, burn him, or throw his carcass into the wild. I don't give a damn. I have no...."

"But Mr. Laurel, it's a sin. They can't remove the dead from their peace..." Mrs. Canes argued and the voices grew dimmer, though they were still there.

Jill went back to her toy box, took the wooden tombstone out and went out into the garden. From the flowers there, she plucked some white daisies, took the ribbon from her hair, and bound them into a bunch. She felt herself slipping into a stew again. Edwin was going to be exhumed and perhaps thrown away in the wild or into a river, or he might be buried somewhere far away. She must put the flowers and fix the marker on his grave. Although she didn't know what use it would be, she knew she had to do it.

"Miss Canes," she called, "they're going to dig him up, aren't they?""

"Oh, Jill! Honey!"

"When?" Jill stared at her sharply, very still.

"Well! Listen..."

"When?" she cried.

The woman knew she couldn't stop the child now.

"They'll be on their way by now, I suppose. Can you please...."

And Jill rushed out. She remembered how well she ran in times like these. With her staggering breath, pounding heart, and strained eyes, she remembered the way she had been, and now was. Her hands clung to the flowers and held the grave marker tightly to her chest. The first drizzling drops of rain kissed her face, but it was still a long way to go, a long and tortuous, gravelly path. If they hadn't made it yet, she would quickly fix the board, put the flowers on the grave and say the prayer.

But what if they reached Edwin's grave before her? What if she found them digging him out when she arrived there? Her heart grew fainter but her pace was as steady. She ran and ran, dodging the bushes and boulders in the hilly ascent.

But the grave never appeared. The drizzle increased. Her tears joined the raindrops. She wanted to get to Edwin's grave, but now she knew she wouldn't make it. She had lost her way again. Her strides shortened and eventually she stopped. She was all in, so she sat on a flat boulder, surrounded by mulberry trees. Rain soaked her and her breath came hard, in and out. Tears ran from her eyes, trickling down her cheeks, finally falling on the wooden board lying in her lap with white daisies on it.

It read: "Only Edwin."

Old Nimi

If you happen to walk along the dusty path leading from the town's green northern fields to the more urban south, at about noon, any day, perhaps you'll see old Nimi heading compulsively down the road to the town's eastern border. Her dark, wrinkled, and skinny figure has a dreamy mien. If you are not looking at her from too great a distance, her small brown eyes will appear to you rather clouded, as if they had been harboring part of the road's dust and smoke. With strained eyes fixed straight ahead, she keeps a slow but determined pace down the road.

In her right hand, old Nimi holds a plastic bucket of faded brown; in her left, she carries a small broom. Add to these her long and loose, shabby-looking skirt, and you have reason enough to guess that she is a sweeper out on duty. But if you follow her some little distance, you will surely conclude that she is not part of the town's cleaning team. Her bucket and broom are of course meant for cleaning, and if you are curious to know where she is heading and why, perhaps you can follow her at some distance. Don't worry about being caught; she always walks after switching her awareness away from the surroundings. Even if her eyes catch a glimpse of you, nothing is likely to happen as long as you keep your distance behind her. Your image will hardly find room in her mind. Things have lost their form for her; only activity shapes her life.

Your walk will not exceed a kilometer at most when old Nimi will enter the town's graveyard for the local riffraff. Just as the open ground near the town's center of residential areas is occupied by people of class, the bushy, abandoned land at the town's southern border was allowed for burying the dead of the less well-off townsfolk. Old Nimi's youngest son, Sabdetz, is buried under a berry tree in the yard's last row of graves.

Through a path trodden across the bushes partly by the cattle and partly by her feet, the old woman will reach her son's grave and sit there near the marker. As you watch from behind a bush or from the corner of the road, she rests her face on the hard, cold marble slab of gravestone right where her son's face would lie a few feet beneath the soil. No heart-rending cries come from her mouth now, as her mourning spirits have been tamed with time. Three years are not too short a time for a bereaved mother to lose her power of loud lamentation. And yet, in the prostration of her body over the grave, you will easily see her never-ending wretchedness. That is what they are like...mothers!

There is no point in trying to offer solace to old Nimi, because the touch of her son's grave is far more anointing than any word of kindness. Neither is it fitting for anyone to intervene in her most precious moment at the final resting place of her flesh and blood by asking her how and why it all happened. Anybody in the town will tell you in a few sentences: that Sabdetz was acting as a mediator between two conflicting parties from the nearby tribal areas, and that someone from one of those parties shot him one night when the negotiations failed to produce the anticipated results for his group. Old Nimi knows all that, but her cursing has long ceased. Maybe she has come to the common-sense realization that the waste of one's time or that of another life—even a thousand lives— will not bring her son back.

If you are not so new in the area, perhaps you have already come to know that there is no law in the town. People kill and escape to the neighboring tribes, which are beyond the government's jurisdiction. But then the law is about punishing the culprit, not resurrecting the dead. What does an old woman get from the wounds and pain of a criminal? She has got enough of her own now. She lacks any impulse of joy or the slightest comfort, except what she can find in the look and touch of her dearest child's final abode.

So there she sits for some time, watering the young man's grave with her tears. Then she wipes her tears with her worn-out shawl and picks up the bucket. She descends the clay slope to the stream, fills the bucket with water, and returns to the grave. Starting at one end, she sweeps all the dust and dirt off its marble frame, making it appear shining white as new. She takes a step back, views the renovated look of her son's grave, and raises her hands to God, praying for the soul that is out somewhere in some remote world. The woman then bends on her knees to kiss her son goodbye till the next day.

You may feel surprised at how old Nimi fails to realize that what she washes clean is not her son's abode but only a stone which covers his dead bones. But that is where you, like everyone else in the town, fail to see through the eyes of the aged woman— eyes that are washed clean with tears of love.

Oubliette

I remember Segal, our aggressive beast of a dog, who lived with my aunt and me. We never let him loose outside the house. Whenever he did somehow get outside, someone came under his wild attack. He did make it outside a couple of times. Once out there, he attacked Ken, the son of our neighbor, Mr. Myer. Luckily I was there on the spot and hit the dog hard enough to get Ken's leg out of his teeth quickly. Otherwise a serious injury would have resulted.

Several days later, when I had him outside for a walk on a chain, he yanked my hand violently and jerked himself free to attack the notorious Brosho's bull terrier, who was calmly advancing at some distance with his master. I was shaken with fear both because Segal, no matter how aggressive, was no fighter, while Brosho's dogs were all trained to be good fighters, and also because I knew that Brosho, being a scoundrel, always had a gun with him. He was a beast in manly form.

I ran after Segal, who leapt ahead, snarling, and who then attacked the neat, white creature head on. The terrier easily grabbed him in his enormous jaws and dragged him around. I entreated Brosho to free Segal and he scolded me angrily, advising me to keep away until the ferocity of the beasts was a little pacified.

We both tried for a couple of minutes and finally pulled our dogs apart. The matter ended without any bitterness. However, Segal's sweet hopes of getting out were done for after that. We wouldn't let him even come near the gate. His freedom consisted only in getting to the roof, from where he could view the outside world. He soon came to relish this new pleasure, and would scamper about each of us, coaxing us into opening the door at the top of the stairs for him. I knew his desire for, and need of, freedom. When I would open the door for him, he would sit up there, close to the edge, and watch the world till someone would force him to come down for his supper. He would come down only reluctantly, and in the morning, he'd start jumping at the first person to rise and come out of his room.

Sometimes a somber thought would take hold of my mind, a grave question on his behalf: *Will Segal die in this prison, always watching the outside from the roof but never again in his life getting free, even for a little while?* I wanted him to get out once more, but I could never trust him. *How could I know he had become a good boy?* The terror that he could arouse kept me from following my plans to take him out for a walk someday on a strong chain.

One day when I returned home from the city, where I had stayed for a couple of weeks, I learned that Segal was dead. My fear had come true. He had died in prison, and his carcass was set free. I was told that he had suffered severe diarrhea, and that he had died on the lawn.

And this left me with an odd sort of wish. *If only he had died on the roof!*

Recreating Stone

The ceremony was glorious. The families of the three late astronauts received honors and grants for the contribution of their dear ones. Ethan Stone was the youngest of those dead in the tragic accident of Nova-3. The 35-year-old exobiologist had investigated remarkable evidence of bacterial life on a moon of Jupiter. In five years, Stone had achieved so much that he became the pride of the nation. With his titles and medals, he was in the news in the papers, on television, and on radio. His family and friends encircled him at gatherings and feasts. Kelly Stone's face shone with joy. Old Mr. Stone and his wife blessed their son with kind smiles. Even little Johnny Stone twinkled in his father's lap with winsome pride.

Then came the news of the terrible accident. On its way back from Jupiter's vicinity, Nova-3 suddenly exploded. Everyone had now seen photographs of the explosion's debris, although no one knew why it happened. A technical fault was their best guess.

The Stones were shaken. Everything was gone. There was no more of the "real" Ethan Stone. His titles were there; the news records were there; the fame was there. But Ethan Stone was no more a real man. He was a legend.

For two months the tragedy was mourned. Then came the ceremony in honor of the scientists. Their achievement was lauded. Family and friends expressed their love and affection for the late heroes. Kelly Stone cried with emotion on the stage, holding little Johnny Stone, who smiled winsomely. A gold medal and a check for five million dollars went with her for her husband's contributions. Mr. and Mrs. Stone told their memories of Ethan as the only and best child they had. And certainly they were filled with pride over his genius. They were both awarded silver shields and the privilege of a standing ovation.

But in a corner of the rows of chairs, Emily Brandon sat oblivious to all that was being said and done. Her face was blank. Her pensive green eyes were fixed on the large photo placed in the center of the stage along with those of the other two astronauts. She was absorbed in Ethan Stone. He was there in his official uniform, bearing a confident expression, a light, dignified smile playing in his eyes and on his lips. His hair was neatly combed to the right and the shallow dimple on his chin made his shaved face even more handsome. He was the man she loved.

* * *

When Emily had told Ethan that she loved him, he had smiled and said, "Well, sure. Thank you, Emmy." And after a pause he added, "But of course I don't have the same passion for you. It's just platonic love, you know. I like you being my cousin."

This was enough to pierce her heart with a pang. Later she hated herself for expressing her love, knowing well that the only thing he had a passion for was his career, his success as a scientist. His love for her, however, didn't vanish from her heart. It was probably because she knew she had no rival.

I'd better leave him alone for a while, she said to herself, *and he'll come to me on his own.*

But he didn't. Two years later, Ethan Stone married Kelly Vasoff, the daughter of a senior scientist. Emily was shattered. She wanted to cry aloud that Ethan was hers. But her sense of respect, her dignity, sealed her lips. She gathered herself bit by bit. Her art of painting was her crutch, and she held on to it. She still loved Ethan, but no longer did she make his portraits. She burned the previous ones, and was determined not to draw him again. She had almost come to terms with her life being that way when he came one evening to see her, to tell her about the space mission. Fear made her heart numb.

"No!" she cried.

"Emily, come on! We'll be safe."

"What if you don't come back?"

"I'll achieve a lot. My family will be proud of what I do."

"Yes." She suddenly had a fit of emotion. "Your wife will be rewarded for your achievement. And your parents, too. They'll get what you can't get them now. But what will I be left with? Tell me, Ethan. What will I get? I won't take even the whole world in exchange for you." Tears welled up in her eyes.

He didn't respond. She knew he wouldn't. And she hated him for it. Only silence filled the seemingly endless moment. Then he said he would leave. She nodded, not looking at him, but fixing the plain gray wallpaper with her strained eyes. He said goodbye. For an instant her eyes darted inadvertently after his face. He had a formal, handsome smile. Her heart was torn. She clenched her jaw and looked away from him. He was gone. She hated him now. The chains of love were broken. She was free at last. And she heaved a cold sigh of relief, relief that slowly enveloped her smoldering heart.

* * *

The ceremony was over. The Stones went to their home and so did Emily. Memories of the past years filled her mind, especially of the time when she was floating along with the precarious hope of a reunion with Ethan, of his coming back and telling her that he loved her. And then she remembered their final meeting, when her tears had failed to stop him, to save him from death. She hated him then. But that was as fleeting as all her previous tantrums of hating him.

Love for Ethan overcame everything in the end. It filled her soon after he had left her. And it was springing in her heart again, ever more intensely. After six years, she was once again taking out her colors and brush to paint Ethan on the canvas.

That night, she didn't sleep. She was absorbed in drawing Ethan, just for herself. With teary eyes and with hands working spontaneously, she was drawing his figure, in his uniform, his arms crossed, his eyes smiling on her. All night long she worked with an amorous heart to create Ethan again, her own Ethan Stone

The Beautiful Six Years

Laboring his legs upstairs in that dingy tavern, Adam Cooper failed to answer the question in his mind. *How could a woman like Nora Reed live in this place?* Naturally, it led to another question. *Did this place cause her death?*

At length, the attendant brought him to a small room in the most obscure corner of the building. He unlocked the wooden door, eaten by termites all along its frame.

"Here, sir," said the attendant, leading him in. Adam felt the warm, stuffy air meeting his nostrils, carrying a mixed smell of wood, carpet dust, and mold.

"Thank you," said Adam, and the attendant left him alone. Closing the door, Adam turned to scrutinize the place where his old friend had breathed her last. He and Nora had had a long platonic relationship bound by mutual interest in books, country music, and antagonism towards conventionality. Unlike Nora, he had some friends, whose society finally induced him to start a family. When he married the young and rich Tracy Brandon, Nora became slowly ostracized. With her thinning hair and emaciating complexion, she suddenly found herself an old doll whose only playmate had changed his taste.

Taking her books and the souvenirs of her youth, Nora Reed left her rented apartment uptown and permanently hired a small room in Stayer's Tavern just outside the city, in the small town of Craigwood. That was six years ago, Adam remembered. He had visited her every couple of months or so and had pressed her to come and live with them in their annex.

"Thank you, Adam," Nora would smile, looking at him. "I'm perfect here!" He had, at times, felt pangs rising in him with every little move of her weak and wrinkled hands as she made him coffee or tea in that secluded haven of hers. They still talked about books, characters, viewpoints, and people. But something vital had changed, was lost for good. He would get over his nameless guilt by reassuring himself of his loyalty to their friendship. She acknowledged it.

"Adam, it's so kind of you to take time away from your life to see me here." Nora would express her gratitude with a soft generosity. But then those very words struck him as if carrying a shadow of discontent. Exchange of gifts had never entered their friendship. It had, from the very start, been a very skin-deep expression of honesty. The moments they had in each other's company served as the unbreakable thread holding their lives at the ends of miles of space.

There was one thing that could break this thread: death. And it finally worked its way between them.

He was then out of the city, staying in Sabestland, fifty-two miles from Craigwood. His wife Tracy and three-year-old son Dave longed to visit Tracy's parents. So Adam took them there for two weeks.

The manager of Stayer's Tavern called early in the morning, with apologies preceding the news of Nora's death.

"Yours was the only number we felt like calling," the manager said.

As the shock of the news faded, Adam wrote the manager a check to arrange for Nora's burial. Next day, he went straight to the church. Nora lay like a clean white doll, self-contained and silent, in the coffin. He could not help crying. A few tears were the only possible words to convey his honesty. The burial took place in the churchyard. He was the last to leave. From the churchyard, he went to the tavern.

"We've locked the room, sir," the manager told him, "but we found this at her bedside. It advises us to hand her belongings to our old servant Amalie. It was she who stayed with her two nights when Miss Reed ran a high fever. Amalie also took her the hospital. Perhaps Miss Reed remembered her service."

Adam read the letter. Nora had left him her meager bank balance and a mirror in her room.

The last item puzzled him. *A mirror!* He asked the manager to let him take a look inside the room. The attendant with the key led him there.

Alone, Adam glanced at the empty room. It had never felt empty like that before. He himself had never felt so empty and lost. His eyes found the mirror on the wall opposite the entrance. He remembered the words in Nora's handwriting in her last letter: *Do not take the mirror off the wall. Let Adam take it himself.* His curiosity ran high.

Why would she leave it to me? he thought, and approached the mirror. It was a small, rectangular glass in a bluish gray plastic frame of dated design. Dust covered the glass.

He took a tissue from his pocket and wiped the dust off its surface. His face appeared in the mirror, clear and distinct. For a moment, he kept looking at the face that stared back at him. There was a striking difference, a thing that left him wondering. The wrinkles of his face and the circles beneath his eyes were not visible now. He looked younger and fresher than he had looked in any mirror over the past many years.

Nora's words filled his thought. He remembered that she had stayed here for six years, never exactly telling her secret reason for staying so long. Moments flew past him and his image in the mirror as they kept looking at each other. Then he slowly woke up and took the mirror down from the wall.

The Bed

"Mom, you can stay here another week at least," says Barbara Keele to the gray-haired old woman gray with a countenance oblivious to grief. She looks at Barbara, her recently widowed daughter, with maternal affection.

"I love being here with you and the kids, dear," says the senior woman, "but you know it's been a month now and Stephen's kids there at our home must be missing me."

"We'll miss you here," Barbara attempts to persuade. She is easy with her mother's presence, especially in her late husband's bed where he spent his last days of illness. Somehow she is not easy with the thought of leaving that bed empty. It feels strange to her even as she thinks why someone must be there in that bed. The last two years of her husband's illness had been awfully burdensome to her: feeding him, bathing him, listening to his nonsense, and helping him urinate, after which the place would become unbearably stinky.

But now when he is gone, the sight of the clean bed during the day bites her. Her mother and two sisters have been staying with her since the first day of Bruce's death. As they speak of leaving, Barbara is more anxious about her mother's absence during the night.

"And besides, dear," continues the placid voice of her mother, "I miss my own bed terribly. You know I am never easy sleeping anywhere except my own bed there in my room. You can do without us, Barbara and that you must, you know."

Barbara thinks of the evening, when the bed will be empty. It occurs to her that she must learn to live that way and so it is time to adjust to the shift in life, an easier life without an ill husband. All she needs is a way of tiring herself to sleep. So she starts thinking of a long to-do list of chores that will effectively replace the absent burden of the care of the her late husband.

In the evening, Barbara's unease looms as she glances at the empty bed. She does not want to ask any of her children to fill the scene. All of them are grown up and addicted to their own sleeping places. As they all retire to their rooms, Barbara sits in her bed, reclined against the pillow, thinking about how to sleep. She looks at the empty bed that reminds her of the dead man and the old woman who had kept the emptiness at bay for some time.

The clock ticks. Barbara has found a way to sleep. By midnight she is in deep down in her dream. The bed is empty no more. The largest picture frame in the room is no longer on the wall. It has been tucked in the bed and covered by a blanket. Little Sean's toys and the consolation cards are lying on the pillow. At the foot of the bed lie some of Barbara's dirty clothes that will be washed tomorrow. Till then, they have found the best place for the night.

The Birds Return

Diane walked along the cheerless corridor of the local hospice, stopping at room number eleven. She pushed the door gently and peeked in, to see whether the old man was awake. As usual, he was, cocking his sunken eyes toward the door. His hearing was perfect, even at this stage of his life, when virtually nothing was left of him that could be called life. Diane entered the room and approached the patient's bed.

"Hello, Uncle Robert!" She placed her hand against the wrinkled cheek of the lean statue. Signs of a lifeless smile of welcome appeared in his dimmed eyes. He responded by attempting to nod. Diane sat on the chair beside the bed. She stopped herself from asking how he was doing. They both knew that he was dying. Age and illness had eaten him away. The cadaverous body rotting in the hospice could be shifted to the inside of a grave at any time. All the doctors awaited were his closed eyes and his still breath.

"Sit," the old man uttered meekly, looking at the space on his bed. Accepting the invitation, Diane left the chair and sat by his side on the bed.

"Yes, Uncle Robert," she said softly, placing her youthful hand on his emaciated one. "I'm glad to see you. I hope you're not suffering much pain now." Diane knew he could not speak much. He looked at her face with a certain questioning look, as if deciding upon something.

Her curiosity and pity grew at once. She thought again about why he would send her a request to visit him on a workday. The old man's questioning look subtly changed into one of affection and trust. Diane smiled for reassurance. His left hand slowly slipped down beneath the bedclothes and came out with a rusty metallic item in it. Diane saw it was a key, one of those old-fashioned keys used to unlock metallic chests, usually made of tin.

"Room, my..." he tried to convey with a faltering breath. Diane took the key from him, nodding with an assuring smile. She thought it was meant to lead her to some kind of will, which her dying great-uncle might have preserved in some old box in his ancestral house. An indefinable peace and indifference covered his face as Diane put the key in her purse.

He kept looking at her with gentle, detached eyes while she spoke words of encouragement that she herself did not believe. As she said she was about to leave, he gently pressed her hand. She bent over and kissed him on his sallow forehead, which was covered with age spots. Exiting the room, she saw him for the last time. He had closed his eyes for sleep. Early next morning, she came to know that he had never awoken again.

* * *

After the funeral, Diane took her Uncle's key and went to the old family house, where one of her aunts lived with an elderly woman who served her. The ladies were happy to see Diane. They spoke about Robert Jones's death.

"I want to see his room, Aunt Becky," said Diane.

"Of course, my dear!" Her aunt led her upstairs to the old man's room and left for the kitchen to make them some coffee.

Finding herself in an old room where her ancestors had once lived, Diane had a strange feeling of time. It was not the old wooden clock that captured her attention, but something non-material, something that felt to her like an invisible bridge between life and death.

She moved slowly across the room, staring at each and every one of its items. Her eyes became fixed upon a medium-sized tin box lying beside the cupboard. Its blue paint would have been bright and fresh in the past, but now its surface looked dull and dingy. Diane walked to it, took the key from her purse, and applied it to open the dusty lock. It worked.

She found the box full of small objects that would please a youthful heart: a baseball cap, a couple of poetry books, gift cards, rings and chains, and some medals. The item that most caught her attention was a black and white photo tucked in the small wooden frame that made up part of the box's internal design. The photo showed four young people, three young men and a girl, all with vibrant expressions and bright faces radiating the liveliness of youth. The young men appeared to be in their early twenties, while the young woman looked a few years older than them. She stood at the rightmost side in the photo, wearing a smile, just like the three young men.

Diane carefully took the photo out of the frame and looked at it closely on both sides. She read the names written on the back of it in black ink that must have once been bright, at the time the names were written. The names were Sarah, Andrew, George, and Robert. Diane gave the photo a closer look and identified her late uncle among the men. Looking at his smooth face and radiant eyes in the photo, a feeling of loss loomed within her heart.

The date on the back of the photo revealed that it had been taken some 46 years before. Diane could not help feeling curiosity about who Sarah, Andrew, and George were, as she had never heard of them before. Clearly, they were not part of the family, given that she knew her relatives. *Perhaps Aunt Becky could tell me*, she thought. Putting the photo in her purse, Diane closed the box, locked it, and went downstairs to the kitchen to ask her aunt about the people in the photo.

***

"Hi! Is this Mr. Tyler's house?" Diane asked the plump, middle-aged woman who stood at the door, looking at her with questioning eyes.

"Yes, it is," she answered. "And you are...?"

"My name is Diane Strob, and I work as a fashion designer." Diane showed her card. "I've come from Elton Town, not on business, but rather a family matter, if I may call it that. May I come in?"

The woman let her in, still looking somewhat confused. She led Diane into a small room close to the kitchen.

"My name is Anna. I'm James Tyler's wife," her hostess told her after they had sat down on the sofas.

"James Tyler is Andrew Tyler's son, if I'm right," Diane guessed.

"That's right," Anna nodded, still wearing a questioning look.

"Mrs. Tyler, I am the grand-niece of Robert Jones, who used to be a close friend and neighbor of Mr. Andrew Tyler in their youth. Robert Jones, my Uncle, passed away two days ago. I found this photo in his private belongings." Diane took out the photo and gave it to Anna. "It shows Mr. Tyler there, standing with Uncle Robert near the potted plant. I had a strong desire to see Mr. Tyler and share this photo with him. Maybe he would like to speak about Uncle Jones. Do you think Mr. Tyler would be happy to see me?"

Anna took her curious eyes off the photo to look at Diane.

"I'm sorry about your uncle, Diane," she said. "Andrew would certainly have been very glad to see you and share his memories of the past. But I'm sorry to tell you that he passed away last week."

Diane sat dumb, letting out a meek "Oh!" A moment of silence passed between them.

"I'm sorry!" Diane finally spoke. "Was Mr. Tyler ill?"

"Yes, he was very ill," Anna gently returned the photo. "He had been suffering from colon cancer for the past eight months. We would visit him daily at the city hospital the last several weeks. On Thursday evening the hospital nurse called to inform us about his death."

Diane did not know what to say. Her attention had shifted to a thought previously unattended to. Maybe all the four friends in the photo were dead by now. She had a feeling that she must find that out as soon as she could.

* * *

Dialing George Steele's number, which she got from a hospital nurse after making a series of calls, Diane sensed a diffused sort of agitation.

"Hello!" The voice sounded like that of a weak, aged man. Diane breathed out part of her stress in a puff. So George was still alive!

"Hello! This is Diane Strob, I'm a fashion designer from Elton Town," she began. "May I speak to Mr. George Steele, please?"

"To George?" asked the fellow, surprise filtering through his tone. It sounded to her the precursor of something not cheerful.

"Yes, um..." She didn't know how to proceed. "This is Mr. Steele's house, isn't it?"

That's right," answered the fellow. "How did you get our number?"

"Well, a nurse at the Convalescence Center gave it to me. I'm actually Robert Jones's grand-niece, sir." Diane realized the need to convey the purpose of her call. "My uncle passed away a few days ago, leaving his personal album to me. I found Mr. George Steele's photo in it. He was a friend of Uncle Jones's. So I thought I should call Mr. Steele and see if I might see him in person to record his memories of my uncle. I'd be thankful if you could allow me to speak with Mr. Steele by phone. May I ask who you are, sir?"

"Well, young lady, I'm George's brother Adrian," said the man in his mature and gentle voice. "Sorry to hear about your uncle's death. George, too, is no longer with us. He departed more than a month ago after living with partial paralysis for three years. Didn't the nurse tell you?"

Diane listened to his words, sitting dumb, thinking about the possibility of Sarah Alcott's death.

"I'm sorry to hear about Mr. Steele's death, sir." Diane fought with somber dumbness, barely managing to speak. Thanking Adrian, she ended the call and made up her mind to find about Sarah as soon as possible.

* * *

It disturbed Diane to know that the three men in the photo were all dead, dying in the same year and at nearly the same time. It appeared as if their lives were abstractly connected. Diane could not help thinking that, if a strange connection did exist, then Sarah would also probably have departed for good.

To her relief, Sarah Alcott was still living, and in reasonably good health. Locating her took Diane several calls and some legwork until she found her in a peaceful and scenic hillside house in Nash Valley. There the old woman lived with her daughter, son-in-law, and grandchildren. When she learned that Diane was Robert Jones's grand-niece, Sarah received her warmly, hugging her in her thin but shapely arms. Her wrinkled face still radiated a sanguine glow and her eyes were bright.

"My God!" exclaimed Sarah upon seeing the old photo showing her youth and that of her friends. "How lovely!" The aching joy of her expression touched Diane's heart.

"Thank you, my dear! Thank you so much! You brought me a treasure no one else could ever have done." Sarah was all joy and gratitude. Though not wanting to becloud her happiness, Diane went on to tell her about her uncle's death and the deaths of Andrew and George. Sarah cried as she looked at the photo and heard the news.

"You know, when we gathered at this place," she began, letting Diane feel the grace of her speech, "it was the day before we all had to leave for different places. Andrew was going to work in textiles in Limberdove. George would leave for Dublin to study European history, and Robert meant to stay at Elton and take care of the family's orchards. And I was going to go to New Verd City to learn nursing. It was a wonderful evening. The four of us took a long walk across the green hills and came to Robert's family orchard where Robert had us photographed. See how nice we all look together!" She looked up at Diane with teary eyes and smiling lips.

"Yes, very lovely indeed." Diane felt an invisible stream of some pure quality that gushed out of the old woman's presence and filled the whole place.

The next moment, Sarah's expression changed to one of deep glumness.

"You know," she said, seemingly lost in her past, "I would contact them whenever I could, and we did all meet a few times, especially on Robert's birthday. He was so generous and caring regarding his friends. I remember we were all a happy company on his fiftieth birthday in Elton. But after that the four of us never got together again. Time just took our lives along its flow. And now...." She stopped, looking lost and oblivious to the need of completing her sentence.

Diane took a seat near her and gently put her hand on the lady's emaciated hands. "Mrs. Alcott, I think you all had an unusual joy of true friendship. While three of your company followed one another closely into another life, I am so happy to speak to you here. I wish you many more years, healthy and happy ones." Sarah's beautiful and peaceful smile returned as she watched Diane speak. Then they embraced each other. Diane asked her permission to leave.

"Can I keep this photo for a little while?" asked Sarah with a friendly confidence.

"Of course!" Diane gave her the photo. "It belongs more to you than to me. I'd like you to keep it." Sarah thanked her, and as she saw Diane to the door, Diane could see her eyes brimming with tears. Diane promised to call her soon and left the house. Her heart was enveloped in a cozy blanket of peace.

* * *

"Mom passed away this morning," Ruth Alcott told Diane in a grief-sodden voice. Diane held the phone, standing still in her living room that cloudy evening. She heard Ruth sob.

"I'm so sorry to hear this!" At length, Diane overcame the stillness. "I hope her death wasn't painful for her. I saw her just yesterday and she looked well enough."

"Oh… yes…" Ruth sounded as if grappling with her urge to cry. "She lay in her bed, looking fast asleep. There was that photo of her in her youth, the one with the three friends of hers, lying on her chest. She talked about it all the time after you left. We found her unusually happy. But I never knew that her happiness would…." Ruth cried.

"I'll be there at the funeral," Diane told her, adding consoling words to try to pacify the bereaved daughter.

* * *

The funeral was over. Diane returned home and sat quietly in her room, staring at the garden across the window. The birds were returning to their homes, nestling together and making noise that sounded like music from another world. Moments passed silently as her thoughts merged with the music of chirping outside.

A picture lit up in her imagination. She woke up from the quiet and reached the davenport, where she worked on sketching her designs. From there, she took an album and started to turn its leaves, looking at each one with attention and care. Her eyes became fixed on a photo showing her huddled among her cronies— two cousins and three friends from her college. She took the photo out, looked at it closely, and smiled in the peace of the moment.

The next minute, Diane slipped her photo into an envelope and placed it safely in the box where she had found her late great-uncle's photo of himself and his friends. She locked the box and closed her palm over the key.

The Blue Fairy

A wedding was in full bloom at a house in a town called Flintberg. The late afternoon sun shone on the guests who formed small groups of various sizes on the lawn. Young women and children went from group to group, but one small boy stood apart, isolated from all the festivities.

He stood at a distance from the lawn, a spot where he wouldn't be readily noticed. He was somewhat amazed at the joy of the people on the lawn, a child wondering why he wasn't part of such an alluring scene.

Then the drum was struck, followed by the melodious trumpet. An exquisitely beautiful damsel dressed in dazzling sky-blue and adorned with gold started to dance on the lawn. Time was bewitched. The boy was enthralled by the rhythm and grace of her movements, and noted how pleased she appeared. She was very proud of her beauty. Her blue, lake-deep eyes followed the twists of her hands. She was the enthusiastic spectator of her own charm. The boy watched her, absorbedly, spellbound. Ladies and children standing before him partly hindered his view. Whatever he beheld was carved like a vignette in his memory—the beautiful Blue Fairy.

* * * *

At another time, a wedding took place again, on this occasion at the house of the dancing girl. It was evening, now, with dark failing to overwhelm the light of life and joy in the mansion. Noise of laughter, chattering, and conversation echoed all around. The boy who was watching her dance on the other evening was also there.

Young ladies, turned into beautiful fairies, were dancing in a circle, all with full flair. But the Blue Fairy wasn't among them. Today she herself was the bride, wearing her wedding dress and sitting amid her sisters and friends. She was going to be married today; she was to leave. Several rituals portraying joy and earnest well wishes were held.

He was tired, so he went to the room his family was staying in. His brother was already in bed, so the boy lay down beside him. He felt himself in a sort of limbo, being pulled by sleep but hampered by some memories, feelings, and the noise outside coming to him along with the light through the gauze in the window.

A roar of noise rose abruptly from the uniform sea of voices outside. He stood up in the bed. The decorated lawn was out there beyond the window. There she was, in her bridal dress. She was the Blue Fairy again, calm and collected, standing in the flowerbed in the lawn to go through the ritual of showing her face to the participants there. Her shiny blue eyes were closed at this moment as was the custom, and her lips were as motionless as those of a statue. Her white face with its blood-red tint looked like a rose in the moonlight.

He was spellbound again. But this time, the magic couldn't sweep away the gloomy sensation of parting from inside him. There was the feeling that she was going to another house forever, that she wouldn't be seen or danced with as often. The moment came when she was to be carried away in the bridal carriage. Tears slipped out of his eyes and trickled down his cheeks: tears of gloom, of departure, of parting. The Blue Fairy was leaving her paradise. She had just become someone else's fairy, forever.

****

It was the house of the boy who was enchanted with the Blue Fairy's beauty and who had shed tears on her departure to her husband's house. He was sitting in his room playing a game with a coin. Suddenly a woman outside started to utter shrieks broken by her weeping. This was surely a sign of death. A wave of apprehension shook his heart. His younger brother came running in, his face pale.

"Auntie is dead," he conveyed in a faint, wavering voice.

His heart began pounding. He went out to the lawn and started to march irregularly around it, in an agonized obsession. "Auntie is dead." That was all he remembered. He was soon sent with his brother to arrange for a vehicle. Then the people were gone. He could not hold himself steady. Soon he got out, crossed the fields running, and came along the road. He came striding to the house where people were going in and coming out.

"Is Auntie really dead?" he asked someone as he stepped in. At that moment mourning and wailing from inside were clearly audible. He just wanted the answer and he got it --"Yes." He never waited for another word of corroboration, turned right back, and went running to his grandparents' house, the house where he had seen the Blue Fairy in her wedding dress. And there he shed tears unchecked. For the first time in life, he frankly made friends with tears.

That night he was alone on the roof of his house. The path to the cemetery was in view. He saw the cortege in the light of the gas lamp leading the procession. Her familiar silhouette was enlivening the white shroud. He started to weep. It was drizzling. The sky was his friend—shedding tears to match his own. The night was slipping quietly away.

****

He suffered jolts as the coach traveled along the rough road. He was on his way home from the university, once again with empty pockets. His mind was working deep inside on his constant reminiscence of his late aunt today: her love, smiling, affection, beauty, her marriage, and then her final departure. Scenes passed before his eyes. He couldn't stop his tears. Crying before people wasn't permissible, so he hid his head in his arm, simulating sleepiness, to rub his tears off. Then he would look out the window at the passing fields.

One question, a single thought, resounded in his mind. She left forever, her body inhumed in the earth. But where did that love go that she had for us?

Time and time again, he tried to find an answer. All he got of it was: "It lives on whenever my thoughts are pleasant, when I feel brave, and when I am able to love."

The Burial

Once again the emptiness of the evening filled her house. She wandered about aimlessly from one corner of the house to another. Her body witnessed its own loneliness as she saw its outline in the form of the shadow that appeared in the lit places of the house. Her mind was engaged in the memories of her dead child, her dead Ruth.

It was more than a week now. She was out of the shock, the denial, and the unbearable grief of her daughter's death. But the feelings of bereavement were only beginning to surface now. Every inch of the house, every article there seemed so strange and empty. She had put Ruth's things all around the house: her clothes, her toys, her books, and whatever little artwork she had created with her small hands and her winsome mind. But with all this simulated presence of Ruth, the little angel was clearly not there. Little Ruth, her only child, was gone forever.

The doorbell rang, waking her from her sorrowful world of thoughts.

Nick, she said to herself and went to the door. It was he, Nick Carter. He stood close to the threshold. She let him in.

"I'll do it for you," said Nick, looking at her with some lingering doubt in his eyes. She nodded lightly and looked down.

* * *

When Kelly Parker told her neighbor Nick what he had to do in exchange for the money that he owed her, Nick was very reluctant. In fact, he refused straight away to do what she wanted.

"I cannot steal," he said. "If I could, I wouldn't borrow money from you."

"This isn't like theft as people know it," she argued. "Please try to understand my position."

"Well, I'm trying to, but I can't be driven to steal. Why don't you try to understand *my* position?" he returned.

Kelly felt hopeless for a moment. How she could make him feel what she was going through, she didn't know. She sounded awkward to her own ears. It was the seventh day since Ruth's death. And here she was, in Nick's flat, trying to persuade him to steal.

"Nick!" She raised her eyes imploringly to him. "Try to see the mother in me, the mother who has lost her only child."

He stopped and looked at her with compassion. She looked so bereaved, so helpless.

Kelly could see that she had conveyed at least part of her necessity to him.

"I don't quite understand why you would want something that you fought to be removed, Ruth. You had a legal battle over that, didn't you?" Nick looked at her with a puzzled face.

"Yes, I did," she answered in a steady voice. "I wanted to end her pain. I wanted then to let her depart in peace, which they didn't."

"But she is in peace now," he said, looking to her for another word of explanation.

"Yes, she is. But all the time that I stayed by her side, seeing her breathe with the machine, I felt there was more to her life." She paused to breathe. "It feels so strange to say that I felt the whole thing to be a part of her. She died a natural death, but I can't get this thought out of my head, that part of her is left there, in the hospital. It haunts me like a ghost. I'm not crazy, Nick. But if I try to get that thing on my own, everyone will call me crazy. And if I don't ever get it, I'll eventually go out of my mind. I know that. I'll give you more money, all that I have. But please bring me the machine. Please!" Tears welled up in her blue eyes.

"Okay, please try to be strong," said Nick, patting her shoulder. "I'll think about it. And then I'll tell you."

"It haunts me, Nick," she repeated. "Please try to decide soon."

"I will," he answered. "I'll let you know by tomorrow night." He took his hand off her shoulder and she left without saying another word.

***

It wasn't hard for Nick to get inside the equipment lab of the hospital. He was a close friend of the head clerk, and Nick himself had worked there for over a year. Entering the hospital, he had a large bag on his back. Everyone knew it as full of cleaning materials. An hour later, when he was coming out of the hospital, some of the cleaning materials in his bag had been replaced by Ruth's life-support apparatus. Kelly was waiting for him in her car at a distance from the hospital. She looked at him with inquiring eyes.

"I got it," he declared as he got in her car.

* * *

It was evening when Kelly's car stopped at the cemetery. Nick was with her. She stepped out of the car with a heavy heart. Nick slowly went with her to the grave bearing Ruth's name. Kelly had already talked to the priest about spending some time alone with her daughter. It was overcast and there was no one around.

For a minute they both stood solemnly by the grave. Then Kelly turned her eyes to Nick. He saw the redness in them, but he could feel that they were close to seeing relief. He took a small hoe out of his bag and started to uncover the grave. The woman stood still as a statue. Only her hand moved to wipe her tears.

"I think it'll do," said Nick, showing her the pit. She looked at his bag. He knew she wanted the last part of her daughter's remains, the apparatus. So he took it out and gave it to her. She knelt slowly, and gently laid the apparatus in the grave.

Her last tears fell over it. Nick touched her shoulder gently. She rose to her feet, turned around to Nick, and looked at his face. He could see now that her eyes were clear and that her face was cleared of its somber veil of grief.

He smiled at her. And she returned it with a deep sigh.

The Child and the Dead

The house is becoming filled with people visiting the bereaved family. The body of the deceased old man rests in a coffin in the hall lit by sunrays filtering in through the window panes. The middle-aged widow has bloodshot eyes. She is still sobbing, patted and pacified by her sisters, whose children are playing out in the yard. Three young men are going through a series of formal embraces and expressions of commiseration over their father's departure. Their fourth brother has not been able to join them in grief, being detained by his work in another city.

The only daughter of the deceased stands aside, looking faint and circled by her cousins, all young girls of nearly the same age. Two elderly women are seated by the coffin, crying and talking. They have lost their only brother, and now they are the only ones of their generation left in the family. They are crying for their brother, and they are crying for themselves. The only daughter-in-law of the deceased is receiving visitors, overseeing the seating of the guests, and tending to the household.

The feeling of losing the old man forever sets the hearts of his kin on thorns. A one-year-old baby walks through the crowd of lachrymose faces. She is holding a piece of bread in her right hand and her wee mouth nibbles at it. Her winsome eyes are fixed on the coffin and the figure lying in it. As she gets close to the coffin, one of the bereaved widow's sisters lifts her up in her arms. The child keeps looking at the man in the coffin. She extends her arm toward him, offering her grandfather his share of bread.

The Fourth Attempt

Wendy checked her voice recorder three times to make sure it was functioning before leaving her flat. She wanted her full share of credit for the upcoming conversation for the main story of the week. Suicide was not a new topic for the readers of *Insight Weekly*. It had been the focus of the main-story pages three times before. A few readers had complained to the editor for accepting stories which caused such chagrin. So the editor had told both her and Stephen to stop writing main stories on things people didn't want to read. Thus, suicide, abortion, drug abuse, and euthanasia were minimized, rendering mysterious murders and precognitive prophecies the finalists for the main story.

Wendy wouldn't have become interested in suicide again if it hadn't been she who confounded a suicide attempt by Pierce Norman. It was, in fact, the thirty-year-old's second attempt at suicide, and this was precisely the point that had helped Wendy save his life.

It had happened some four months ago. That evening, Wendy left work early due to a headache, and she saw Pierce at a drugstore along the road. Their eyes met, but of course he didn't know her. She merely recognized his face as one she had seen somewhere before. But hardly ten seconds had elapsed when she turned her back to the druggist. The hint had flashed electrically in her mind: *Suicide Attempt Fails; Thirty-Year-Old Pierce Norman Saved*. She remembered his photo, too. The rest was strung very shrewdly in her mind, then and there: a suicidal man and a drugstore made an awfully dangerous combination. Wendy loved psychological thrillers, and more than that, she was always looking for some in real life.

When she alerted the druggist to the possible danger, he told her that he had sold the man some tranquilizers—prescribed, of course. Wendy rushed after him. Asking passersby along the way, she finally caught him in a bathtub in Bingo's Spa a moment after he had taken eight pills and had made the first cut on his left wrist. When Wendy broke in, Pierce looked at her in wonder and disbelief with ensuing protestation. And when she went to see him in the hospital, he again had that question of protest in his eyes: *Why did you do this to me?*

Wendy felt more awkward than happy that she had saved his life. She shared this with Stephen.

"Don't try to be a heroine," he replied, "and if you do, always keep in mind that it's a real life shooting." Such an icicle he was! But surely he was right. No one seemed to admire what she had done so cleverly.

She decided to make it a main story. The editor turned it down coolly.

"I'm afraid it's too sucky to be the main story," she had told her.

"What do you mean?" Wendy was angry.

"I mean it's trite. Don't you understand?"

"Trite! Oh, yeah! And what do you think people need to know? What do you think the druggists need to know and the Bingo's staff needs to know? That guy can make a third attempt. The story could save his life, perhaps more lives."

"Let him make a third attempt. If he does, I'll let you go for the story. I promise."

Wendy told Stephen, "I'd never wish him to make a third attempt." Stephen nodded.

"You think I'm worried about the story and my name over it, in bold?" she asked with an overt expectation of hearing a big "No" from him.

Stephen posed a question in return. "You care for him?"

"Yes, what else!"

"Then I'm afraid you shouldn't have saved him."

Stephen turned and went out, leaving her pondering the tragedy of reason. Pierce Norman was put under outpatient observation for fifty days and he did excellently. Admitting his wrong, he assured them optimism in the future, and came out an apparently different person. He called Wendy to Paul's Café and thanked her for her benefaction, excusing himself at the same time for the trouble he had caused her.

Wendy had jumped to another idea. If she could make Pierce Norman willing to narrate all that drove him to suicide attempts, a more attractive story could be created; sometimes people were more interested in first person narratives than in hearing about other people. Even the editor would be more likely to give this a chance. Wendy didn't express this then and there for courtesy's sake, but she called Pierce the same evening. He said he'd think it over, and she could call him two days later. Wendy was once again excited.

She told Stephen. He just pouted at her. She jumped to hear the editor say, "All right. Try it for the next week but not later. Got it?"

She couldn't wait for the evening and went straight to Pierce Norman's apartment to see him. He wasn't home. His neighbor, Evelyn Smith, informed her that she had seen him going out half an hour before with his dog Bunny, toward the lake. That, in her opinion, was fairly unusual, because he was known to be sleeping at home during these hours.

That much was enough for Wendy. She took her bike and raced to the lake. The spirit of adventure was pouring in on her. A real life thrill! Bunny was alone, standing anxiously beside the water, gazing at it and barking in a protesting tone. Upon seeing Wendy, he moaned humbly. The turbulence in the water and the emerging bubbles revealed that she was there in time. Not wasting another second, she dove into the lake, found Pierce tied to a stone by a rope, wearing a bright red shirt that increased his chances of survival, for it could easily be caught sight of from a distance.

Because of her profession, Wendy always carried a sharp-bladed cutter in her pocket, for cutting out articles. In about a minute, she managed to bring Pierce to the surface. He was unconscious as she began artificial respiration. When he finally breathed, Wendy heaved a sigh of relief.

He didn't regain his senses for the next 34 hours. Wendy told the police that she didn't think it was a suicide attempt. Of course she didn't mention the business of the stone and the rope. Divulging this in her story would be much more effective in stealing the credit and personalizing the matter. Not to mention the pains she took to get to the lake again and take the rope away, burn it completely, and dispose of the ashes. All this engaged her quite enthusiastically. The account was cooking up portentously; she thought her story, once it was printed, would be a bombastic and telling addition to a topic which was rather touchy for many folks.

Her plan for the divulgence of the third attempt was jostled, however, when it was given out by Evelyn Smith that Pierce must have made a suicide attempt. It was soon the gossip roaming about. The local newspaper printed a story on Pierce Norman titled "Suicide or Accident?" and Wendy was distracted. But still, people weren't sure, and since she was keeping the "real thing" in her head, she was pretty much hopeful about her success in dramatizing the series of events. Shooing away the journalists (some were calling her from outside the town) and boring the police with the same made-up story that she had taught Pierce on her meeting with him after he regained his senses, Wendy managed to keep her would-be story going.

The police had failed to find any evidence of suicide either by the lake or in it. They conformed to the truth as described by Pierce and Wendy that Pierce had become dizzy while fishing and had fallen in the lake, then losing consciousness. Evelyn Smith was issued a notice, warning her to stop spreading any sort of rumors about the young man, and Wendy saw herself smiling before the mirror in her bathroom. The story was still Go.

Pierce met her four times after the third attempt. He didn't utter anything other than formalities, and he never thanked her for saving his life this time. She thought that he considered all her concern merely part of her story. So she called him to ask for a meeting. He said he'd think it over. Meanwhile, Wendy asked Stephen to do something about the coming week's story, because she wouldn't be able to make hers in time.

Stephen was usually the person who brought her any bad news. This time it was worse news. The police department had decided to present her with a special medal for saving Pierce Norman's life twice. The annual ceremony was supposed to be held on the 25th of the current month, a day before her story would come out. How very awkward it would be to get the medal one day and then be summoned for accomplice in fabrication the next day.

She didn't know what to do. She remembered herself saying, "This is not happening!" But then the solution wasn't hard to think out; she must find some way to be busy on the 25th.

Meanwhile, Pierce Norman was doing well. He called back to say he was ready to have a talk with her, though he didn't tell her the time. Meanwhile, Wendy ordered her jumbled set of writings, jacketed it, and wrote down her manuscript of the story, typing it on her Macintosh. And then weird gossip began to travel around town. Within two days, local skepticism was growing regarding the sincerity of Pierce Norman in his suicide attempts. That is, they thought he didn't want to die, probably because he feared death, but simulated suicide attempts in order to get attention and fame. In other words, his were false attempts.

This was both interesting and important for Wendy. People could float that way and then she would haul them back with a jerk by revealing the actual desperation that drove him to his death wish. Here, she stumbled upon her own folly. Up to now, she had never actually attempted to make him tell her about the anguish that was constantly distracting him from life.

Then luck blessed her generously, just in time. Pierce called. He asked her to come over for a discussion the following evening. Also, he had become aware of what people were spreading around.

"Maybe they're right," he laughed bitterly on the phone. "If I had wanted to die, I'd have been dead by now." Wendy tried to console him, though she knew she wasn't good at it. Of course she remembered to ask about the time of meeting. Seven o'clock. All right!

She was ready now, with her recorder and a jacket of papers all about story, including a short questionnaire jotted down roughly, and her camera loaded with a new roll of film. So she was all ready to set out to Pierce Norman's house for the most exciting story of her life.

* * * *

Pierce, looking paler than before, received her normally. He had coffee already made, and they took the table in his living room. He looked to her to begin the conversation.

"So how are you?" she began, slowly pressing the record button inside her purse. She didn't want to miss a single word.

"You see me before you," came the dry reply.

"Well," she pouted. "I think you've come to terms with life finally. You look better." But she didn't believe her own words. She thought that was what she ought to have said. His face was almost blank, his eyes glum. He replied with a "Hum." It was getting awkward. Wendy tried a platitude, saying, "Well, life's really beautiful, if you're willing to see it that way." Fearing a gap in the conversation, she continued, "And that's why I'm here, to share this feeling with you. Will you tell me your picture of life?"

He fixed on her face starkly. She tried to retain her smile. And then he suddenly said, "I don't agree." He was looking straight into her eyes. "What makes life really ugly is this notion of universalizing the life-is-beautiful cliché. I don't accept it." He sounded like a rebel. Wendy had some idea of what he was like, and knew that she could not let him steer the talk away from what was relevant. So there was this familiar, and feasible, way of short questions.

"Tell me, Mr. Norman," she started, "exactly how old are you?"

"Very old indeed." He looked down, laughing, and then with a sigh he looked back at her. "Thirty years, seven months, and a couple of weeks."

"Where is your family? Your parents, siblings, cousins, etc.," she was quick in asking.

"Repudiated." And so was he.

"Where, if I might be allowed to know?" she requested.

"Kentucky."

"And your love relations? I mean, any girlfriend, or—you know?"

"My soulmate died six years ago. I won't tell you her name or any details." He went glum.

"Right." Wendy reminded herself of the lesson of keeping empathy at bay in order to obtain a good story. Observing a brief, silent pause, she said, "If you could only tell me how…" She broke off deliberately.

He looked at her with scanning eyes. "Suicide," he said, narrowing his eyes with a frown.

"Oh, I am sorry!"

He didn't answer. Wendy waited for him to speak.

"You know," he said, staring out the window, "fear of death is tame in comparison with unending desolation. All I can see is chaos. All I can hear is my own breath. All I can fell is a hollow, servile mess of platitudes, and that's it." He looked at Wendy and asked, "So what exactly is life?"

"It's worth living, Pierce, I assure you." She could say only this much properly.

Then she added, "If she were alive, would you live?"

"Yes." He spoke confidently this time. "But she is not."

"You may..."

"I would not look for a surrogate. It's not business, Miss Peters," he stymied her. "Besides, I did it because of my death, not hers. I want death. Do I have a right to choose when and how to end my life, Miss Peters? Do I?" He was all protest in his question. Wendy sighed, not knowing what to say other than "I suppose so."

"Then why don't you let me have it?"

Wendy was getting distracted. The questionnaire was growing stale in her lap. But she felt she should let things float for the moment.

"Because I can't," she replied. "I want you to come back to this world, this beautiful world."

"Which makes a really ugly tomb," he prompted in a stewing tone. She was answerless again.

"The life you are seeking gets to another one, one as ugly as this." She was getting over it now. "If you are heading for heaven, I'm afraid suicide isn't the route."

"I'm an atheist."

"So am I, but I believe in amelioration, improvement. Join me. We'll be a good team." She smiled to relieve the stress of battle.

"Do you know why I've called you here?" he asked, staring sharply at her face.

"I'd like to hear that from you." She was curious. The crux of the story was perhaps coming up.

"To share something a priest won't share with God." His eyes narrowed a bit. Wendy leaned forward, elbows on the table. She was calm on the outside but was all thrills in her nerves.

"Miss Peters," he paused for a few seconds, staring at her, and then looked out of the window, "I fathered a child. It was a girl." A moment of silence passed; he still looked out. "After my love died, Bonnie was eight months old," he told her with teary eyes.

Wendy was absorbed in his expression as Pierce continued.

"Bonnie had her mother's eyes and lips, and her face. Well, she was all her mother. I thought I could live for her. She was my life transformed from her mother into her. So I had a reason to live. At eleven months of age, she fell off a chair in the nursery, damaging her brain, and went into a coma." He paused and sighed. Wendy was all ears, with a part of her mind saying that the story was going as well as possible.

Then he looked at her again. "I couldn't see my love suspended between life and death. That is when the meanings of the terms were switched. The doctors held out only about a five percent chance of her living, and even then with the certainty of no movement, speech, or sight for her. And there I was, the sole spectator of my dying love, my dying life. My case for euthanasia was rejected. I was expected to catch at the straw of hope in the fathomless, dark ocean of despair." He paused again.

Wendy was growing distracted; the real life story of Pierce Norman was taking over. His account shed anguish that she had failed to feel heretofore. Depths of misery were surfacing. He grimaced and came out of the rush of his excruciating tragedy. Looking at her, he went on saying, "I waited for three months. Her condition deteriorated. So one evening, I..." he closed his eyes, clenching his teeth. Then, relaxing with a sigh, he said, "One evening I killed her."

A pang shot through Wendy's whole being. Then she felt hollow and numb.

"Oh!" She couldn't control her exclamation. "I'm sorry! I really am."

Tears trickled down his cheeks. He wiped them off with his hand. "It's not that I killed her and got away with it," he kept looking outward, his face shining now as if washed clear of the anguish, for a moment, by his own tears. "There's more to it. I killed myself too. I died right there with her. I don't even remember how I spent all these years. It's all a horrible dream of emptiness, emptiness of heart, of being. I thought much of convincing myself to stay, to gain life, but then life means the other state."

He looked at her. "My decision is based on both rational thought and emotional grounds." He was rather placated now. "Please let me go this time! Will you?" he suddenly begged her. It was something she hadn't anticipated. And it was dreadful to hear that. She was taken aback. The inquietude had suddenly leapt up. She didn't know what to say. But then she had to.

"I know your life is a cry of pain. I can feel it," she said earnestly, "but I won't let you die, if I can help it."

"You won't?" he frowned with a stern look.

"No, I won't. Never." She was determined. And suddenly she faced something extremely unexpected. With a quick movement of his right hand he took a gun from his coat.

"If you won't let me die, then you have to face something more terrible than this," he roared, pointing the gun at her.

"No, please! Don't shoot me!" This was all the cold, shivering Wendy could say. But he looked furious. With his gun pointing at her head, flames of vengeance sparkled in his eyes.

* * * *

When the police reached Pierce Norman's house, it was dark. A slight drizzle had made the breeze colder. Two cars stopped in front of his house and five officers got out, guns drawn. Evelyn Smith peeked out from her window to see what was going on.

The scene was indeed thrilling. Wendy Peters was standing helplessly just outside Pierce's front door, her arms tied behind her, her lips sealed with tape, and her eyes red, shedding helpless tears. Pierce's strong arm gripped her neck, and a shining black gun was pressed against her temple from behind. Her muffled cries were just audible. She was a hostage. The police moved into position immediately, loudly crying out their message in order to make Pierce surrender.

"You move and I blow her head off!" Pierce shouted in turn.

They were confused, looking at one another and then him. Wendy was struggling to get out of his grip, but in vain. Neighbors had started to come out on the avenue, and were watching the scene with surprise and concern.

"What do you want?" shouted an officer, to stall for time.

"You. To see her die," Pierce answered indignantly.

"Let her go and tell us your demand," the officer asked him.

"She won't let me in peace," he growled. "I'm going to kill the bitch in front of all of you." His eyes were red, burning with vengeance.

"Good heavens!" a lady among the neighbors cried.

"What do you mean?" The negotiator simulated confusion.

"She seized my right to die, so I seize hers to live. We must get even." He was all threat.

Wendy shook herself forcefully. The drizzle had increased, and so had the heat of the scene. The negotiator kept quiet for a few seconds and then said, "Don't be a fool. Killing her won't let you die. You'll have a long, safe life in jail. What do you think?"

Pierce gazed at him with a stern face, and then uttered a grim "No." With this he whirled the girl around, still clenching her neck. With the other hand he pointed the gun at her head. Wendy shook violently. The police were alert in their positions.

"That's the end of her!" he cried aloud, and pressed the trigger. Two guns were fired at the same time, one bursting his head and the other his shoulder. Five or six rounds were shot. Pierce fell down with blood gushing out of his body. The floor was red with it.

Police rushed to them. Wendy watched Pierce in a trance. He was still alive, looking at her with blood in his eyes. She collapsed on her knees, all in.

"He's dead, sir," one of the policemen called out, after groping him thoroughly. Wendy was rid of the tape.

"You all right?" the negotiator asked. She sobbed audibly, tears trickling down her cheeks. They let her hands free, trying to comfort her. Pierce was dead.

The negotiator picked up Pierce's gun from the floor. "Oh, shit!" he exclaimed. "It's empty." He looked at the dead man and then at Wendy in astonishment. "What the hell was this all about?" he asked, almost in a state of shock. It was raining now. She covered her face and sobbed.

* * * *

"The Fourth Attempt" was the talk of the town for more than a week. Wendy was famous, very famous indeed, as some papers adopted the story and her name flashed before the readers everywhere. She was interrogated by the police, interviewed by reporters, and awarded a medal for saving Pierce's life twice. But all this didn't amuse her anymore. She threw the medal in the lake, secretly of course, and burned all the original writings and the cassette relating the story. She just wanted to forget this incident.

Two months later she was to leave for the neighboring town. *Insight Weekly* had made progress. It was going to start its second office, and Wendy was to manage it there.

Stephen was jealous of her success. "I think this involves a lot of coincidence," he said, "and very little of your conscious effort." Wendy smiled and nodded.

That evening, before leaving town, she went to Pierce Norman's grave and put some flowers there. After observing a few minutes of silence, she returned. And when she was leaving the town behind in her newly bought car, most of the things in town were absent from her mind, left behind.

In her mind was the last look in Pierce Norman's eyes, fixed on her before he died. It was of victory, and peace.

The Shake-Up

Vanessa drove the car past Ronny's Patisserie and turned it onto Packard Street, about a kilometer from Grace Medical Clinic, where they were heading. Reclined passively in the front seat, Sherry had been looking out the window for most of their travel.

"How are you feeling?" Vanessa asked, casting a brief glance at her. The veil of gloom covering Sherry's face seemed to ask another question, one without a voice. Vanessa wanted to hear it, though she knew that answering Sherry's questions convincingly was not possible for her.

"Strange." Sherry persisted in staring outside. Her tone was faint and dry.

"Why? In what way?"

"You drive a lot," she looked at Vanessa and continued," but it's strange to think that the thought may never have occurred to you."

"What thought? Tell me." Slowing down a bit, Vanessa changed the gear to pass another car. Sherry resumed looking through the window glass again.

"The way we move in a car, everything seems to rush past us. The whole world runs past us while we head on..." she paused for a second and then muttered, "always opposite."

Vanessa did not comment.

"Which makes me wonder," Sherry continued, "if it's quite natural for the world to thwart us and equally natural for us to always move across it." Her stare through the glass had deepened.

"People do follow us," said Vanessa, keeping the pace comfortable.

"And we have to turn to see them, only to have all the same again." She sighed and blinked.

"Well, why always get caught in this front and back dichotomy?" Vanessa argued. "Why not take a look sideways?"

Sherry looked over her left shoulder to eye her friend's face. Their eyes met and a smile passed between them. "You're a gift to me, a dear one." Sherry's dim eyes sparkled with a momentary brightness.

"Compliments!" Vanessa chirped. "Did Brent call last night? Or this morning?"

"Yes." Sherry again stared through the window. "At about 11:00. I was in bed. We talked for some twenty minutes."

"Did he insist?"

"Not much. I told him it was final."

"Was he angry?" Vanessa cast her a sidelong glance.

"He wasn't. But he made it clear that he wasn't going to think about having another kid in his life again. I didn't answer that."

"And what about marriage?" Sherry let silence fill the moment.

"He won't talk of it now," she said at length. "I think we need more time to get to know each other better."

Vanessa could not help noticing the uncertainty ringing in her tone, not missing at the same time the slight grimace in her expression.

"I hope the two of you get that soon." Silence filled the rest of their drive until they reached the clinic.

"Here we go!" Vanessa stopped the car. "You want me to come and stay with you?" Vanessa offered as Sherry slowly got out of the car and stood by its door.

"No, I'm okay. Thanks, Vanessa!" She smiled in gratitude.

"Just give me a ring if there's anything, okay?"

"Sure, see you!" Sherry turned towards the entrance of the building.

* * *

Unexpectedly, Brent came to see her while she was in bed about two and a half hours after the abortion. He had brought flowers and a fruit basket.

"I'm glad to see you well," he expressed, caressing her chin.

"'I'm glad you came." She let the tears well up in her eyes. Brent kissed her softly on her cheek. They did not speak.

"Let me take you home," he proposed.

"Vanessa is going to be here in the evening. I need to rest here till then." Sherry drew in a deep breath.

"Right." He blinked. "I'll come. Just give me a call when you're ready."

"I trust you," Sherry smiled faintly to him.

He returned the smile with a touch of compassion and gently spoke. "I wish you could trust the world as well."

A haze of loss clouded her eyes and she heard herself saying, "So do I."

Brent changed the topic at once to his job. He told her about his new dog, his cousins in Rotterdam, and life activities running at the moment. He left after an hour and Sherry closed her eyes to sleep.

Upon waking, she found Vanessa sitting by her bed, reading a magazine.

"I think you're well enough to leave, right?" Vanessa was always so caring.

"Yes." Sherry looked at the clock.

"Great! I've invited Brent to a home-cooked dinner tonight." Vanessa started to collect up Sherry's belongings. "You'll be perfectly at ease, so no fantasies about a Nightmare at Vanessa's!"

"I'll be fine," Sherry replied, sitting up in bed and feeling the first breath of a new life.

***

Two months later, they were observing Sherry's birthday in her flat. Only Vanessa and Brent were there with her.

"Dare I ask how old you are now?" Brent set the stage for expostulation.

"Much older than you can guess." Sherry made the cut in the cake and received felicitations.

"Many happy returns of the day!" Vanessa held her by the arm. "And this for you." She gave her the present.

"You're so sweet!" Sherry gave a smile of admiration. Then she looked at Brent. He held his present silently out to her, with his familiar, unfailing softness meant especially for her.

"Thank you!" Sherry took the gift with a look that acknowledged a sort of condescension.

"Wow! It tastes fantastic!" Vanessa had started nibbling at the cake.

Sherry pitied the cake. "Poor it!"

"Huh?" Vanessa cast her a questioning, slightly protesting glance, while still chewing a mouthful.

"Poor for being so short lived," said Sherry, laughing. Vanessa feigned an angry look.

"It's nice!" Brent took a bit. "I offer you girls a birthday ride in my car."

"You're great, Brent!" Vanessa flew high. "I need to get to the mall, Fashion Chic, you know. You guys would be angels if you could wait half an hour there for me."

Brent looked at Sherry. She was watching his face, looking right in his eyes.

"Well, all right, but..." And Vanessa's loud "Whew!" stifled him.

* * *

Brent and Sherry sat in the car as Vanessa ran inside The Dallies.

"Hi," Brent broke the silence, glancing at her. She responded with a faint smile.

"Can I get you anything?" he asked.

"Be here. That's all." Sherry looked at his hands on the steering wheel. Suddenly an intense desire sprang up in her heart, the wish to speak to him about everything before Vanessa returned. She wanted to clear all the haze lying between them.

"You want to say something?" he asked in a soft and placid voice.

"There's so much that it may take a lifetime," she said, rubbing her engagement ring, trying to suppress her shakiness.

"Well, that sounds affordable." His eyes shone. Sherry breathed out a lifeless laugh.

"Then let's start with you," she said, trying to sound lively.

"I..." He paused as if thinking what to say, then heaved a sigh and started again. "For me, you come first, and you know that."

Sherry remained silent, diverting her stare to the windshield.

"My father always wanted me to be a renowned scientist, but I couldn't make it," Brent continued, "although I did manage to be a successful person, a well-off editor, having good friends, and above all, having you. I want this joy of life to continue in our name, in an ever-increasing way. You know all that." He fixed on her face. Sherry bit her lip.

"And you know about me, Brent," she started. "My mother committed suicide when I was nine. Dad abandoned me to my aunt, whose treatment of me made me run away and wander from place to place, till I was adopted by Mrs. Ashbrook. But the running never ended, and I never got a chance to rest. Now I want to end it." Brent felt the air of desperation in her tone.

"Why not end this fear in your life?" he said mildly.

"This fear *is* my life, Brent." She looked outside. "Ending it will end me. It's like committing suicide without ceasing to breathe. I can't die twice."

Silence lingered for a few minutes. Brent bent over the steering wheel, putting his head on it, covered in the circle of his arms. Ripples of worry ran over Sherry's face.

"You feeling all right?" she asked, softly, with a trace of guilt.

"Um...yeah," he muttered, and then lifting his head to look at her, he said, "I'm happy as long as you're around. You're right. Life's frail, confoundedly frail. Bringing a child into this world is perhaps a crime, but I don't know why I still want you to conquer this monster of fear that our child will suffer just like you did, and just like millions in this world suffer. But you're right in your own regard. I love you, Sherry. I want to be with you, without kids if you like. I'll always be there." Sherry put her hand under his jaw, cupping his cheek. He placed his hand over hers, caressing it for reassurance.

* * *

"Will doesn't bug you, does he?" Angela Penn inquired about her little son.

"Oh, no! Of course not!" Sherry smiled, putting her glass of wine on the table. "We really have a nice time together." Angela smiled happily at this.

"Well, you must have noticed how eccentric he is," said Angela, "inheriting his habits from his father. He just won't listen to me and I can be anything but harsh to him. He has refused to go anywhere to read but with you."

"I'm happy I'm teaching him." Sherry shared her feeling about the child. "As for his eccentricity, it only makes him sweeter. For him, however, I'm afraid it might be dangerous sometimes."

"Oh, Sherry dear!" Angela sighed. "He has death hovering over his head all the time, you know. Falling out of bed, hurting his limbs, sinking in the pool even! The police once interrogated me about his wounds, suspecting me of abusing him. The worst thing is that every accident makes him ever more intrepid." Sherry felt a wash of low spirits for a second.

"Did you seek treatment for his hyperactivity?" she asked.

"Well, he is being treated." Angela sounded as though she were complaining. "But it seems to be ineffectual. Suddenly a wave of concern flashed over her face. "Dear me! Why hasn't he come yet? I'll go see if he's all right." Angela stood up.

"Yeah, sure." Sherry took the glass off the table.

Three days later, Sherry was teaching Will his science lesson in the evening.

"Why do they shock us?" Will's question nearly sounded like a protest, as he pointed at the electric wires in the figure in his book.

"They pour their energy into us suddenly. That's why we feel the shock," Sherry explained. "Tell me, have you ever had such a shock?"

"Oh, yeah! The toaster," he started in a somewhat manic manner. "Once I was in a hurry for the toast and Mom wouldn't listen, so I took the spoon and tried to pull one slice out. Suddenly I fell back like something just threw me there with force." To act out the event, he threw himself back on the couch. "And this is the shock. The spoon must have touched the wires inside the thing, right?"

"Right." Sherry couldn't help laughing at his acting out the receipt of an electric shock.

She looked intently at Will's face. It shone, shone with life. As she watched, he tore the title page off his workbook.

"What are you doing?" Sherry reproved him gently. He pouted and put the thing down, chanting indifferently.

"Now go over there and bring me the stapler from the davenport," she ordered him. He rushed to it and returned with the same vigor. Sherry took the stapler from him and stapled the detached page to the book.

"Interesting!" Will's attention was focused on the stapler.

"Don't tear any page again, understand?" she said and gave him the stapler. "Put it back over there."

"Does it work on a hand?" he asked, putting his forefinger in it.

"Will, don't!" But her worried warning reached him after he had pressed the device hard on his finger.

"What are you doing?" Sherry bent forward, her heart beating fast in fear.

"It worked!" He looked at Sherry, smiling in pride. "It doesn't hurt much, does it?"

Sherry gazed anxiously at his finger.

He put the stapler down and showed his finger to her. Fresh red blood gushed out of the wee hole cut in it.

"Look what you did" Sherry gasped anxiously. "Come with me!"

"But it doesn't hurt," he insisted.

"Come!" She took him by the arm to the dressing table and took out some hydrogen peroxide. "Never do that again! Never!" Anger flew into her tone as she felt the pain, the pain he did not feel.

* * *

It was past midnight. She stood by the window looking outside. Sleep did not touch her tonight. She had just called Brent, telling him to marry her soon. She told him she would like to have babies, at least one of them. A baby of her own. He was overjoyed to hear this and promised to take her to dinner tomorrow.

Then Vanessa called, informed by Brent of Sherry's decision. She too was very happy about the news.

Standing at the window, Sherry turned her head to see the hair drier lying on the carpet with its wire showing bare. An hour before she had had this electric shock that shook up her entire being. She had scraped the wire bare and then touched it with her thumb after switching it on from the mains. A light shriek was what she had uttered but she knew she had expelled a lot, probably all she thought she had by now. Will's face came to her mind.

"It worked!" His voice echoed and she laughed by herself.

"Yes, it worked. Thank you, Will!" She opened the window to feel the breeze.

The Tidings

Stephanie waited for a couple of minutes at the door. Finally someone came to open it. It was an old woman with most of her hair gray, some of it white. Her body was lean and her face appeared weak with age. There were wrinkles on her face but her light blue eyes were clear and carried a faint shine, perhaps of the seasons she had seen.

"Hello! Are you Mrs. Packard?" Stephanie asked. The old woman looked at her intently and then nodded slowly.

"Yes," she said. "Who are you?"

"My name is Stephanie Marker. I... I'm your grandson's friend." A lie came out of her almost spontaneously.

"Jason!" the woman exclaimed with a smile that deepened her wrinkles.

"Yes, we work together in the Intelligence, you know." She did have to speak at least some truth, to pave the way for the necessary one.

"Oh, come in!" Mrs. Packard let her in. Stephanie stepped in slowly. The cottage was small and tidy.

"Do you live alone, Mrs. Packard?" she asked.

"Yes." Mrs. Packard led her into a lounge where a table stood with three chairs around it. The furniture was old but clean.

"Sarah comes three times a day," she said as they took their seats at the table. "She does the cooking, cleans the house, and stays for the night." Mrs. Packard's hands were on the table. Stephanie could see they weren't strong, perhaps never had been.

"Sarah?" She looked at the old woman.

"Yes, the neighbor girl. Tell me about Jason." She suddenly turned to the subject of her grandson. "How is he? Isn't he coming today? He remembers his birthday tomorrow, doesn't he?" Eagerness surfaced on the old face. Stephanie could feel herself at the threshold of a challenge.

"Well, I'm afraid he's too busy this time, like all the rest of us," she started to make up. "That's why I'm here, to tell you that he won't be coming, at least not this time."

"Oh!" Mrs. Packard tried to laugh, and succeeded a little. "I see. Well, I do hear these horrible things on the radio every night. Jason is all right, isn't he?" Suddenly she sounded to Stephanie like a horrid old thing ready to bite her.

"Oh, yes!" She felt the hollowness of her voice. "He's okay but too busy, always engaged, you know. It's a never-ending story, taking care of these bad guys." She forced out a laugh.

"It's okay," replied the old woman in a kind tone. "I celebrate his birthday even when he's not here. And until this day passes peacefully, don't tell me anything bad even if it's there. It's the only day I celebrate now. Why don't you stay for lunch?"

"Uh…" Stephanie's mind was plodding its way to conveying the tidings. This was hard on her now. "No thank you, Mrs. Packard. I think I'll be going now. Jason wanted to know if you needed money." She thought of the compensation in her purse.

"Tell him I'm doing great." She stressed the last word. "Just keep it for the kids he'll have one day," she laughed. To Stephanie it sounded as if her laughter came from somewhere far off.

"Okay." Stephanie stood up. "Goodbye, Mrs. Packard, and take care."

"Thank you for coming." Mrs. Packard accompanied her to the door.

Stephanie gave a final smile and went out. The door was slowly closed behind her. For a while she stood quietly, thinking how long to keep the news of Jason's death to herself. Then she walked to her car. She had more than 24 hours to work it out.

The Words

Just like he reads "The End" on every classic book's last page, he knows that the story of his own life will come to "Finis" one day. What he doesn't yet know, and what has till now saved him from the consternation of perishing, is the exact time of his end in the undefined future. He is glad to be unable to determine that moment for himself, while wondering at the same time over the audacity of those who do so. Very often, his thinking retrieves the words *foolish*, *crazy*, *coward*, and sometimes *brave*, whenever he makes a conscious dive into the imaginary situation of a young man just about to blow out his brains with his gun held tightly against his temple. As the finger of the man presses the trigger, a screen of darkness covers Fred's imagination and one or more of the words associated with suicide appear on the dark screen: *foolish*, *crazy*, *coward*, *brave*.

Though he's been trying not to think of his death, the thought of his own end has been teasing Fred for several months. He doesn't remember when or how it started. Even this is becoming a poking question for him, and he sometimes suspects that some subconscious choice of his own may have invited the ghastly thought of dying. The news of someone's death by accident or any unexpected chance event sends shivers up his spine. Whether in company or alone, the word *death* has become the trigger of a dismal train of thought that always gets lost in the endless screen of darkness.

Also accompanying his dread is a modicum of never-ending curiosity about what it will feel like to be dead. The screen of darkness again covers his imagination except for the faint glimpse of a coffin lying on the bank of an empty grave while the feet of people can be sensed behind the haze enveloping the ground. What will it be like being dead, with no breath or heartbeat? The ensuing rush of darkness is truncated with a whiff of laughter. Lying dead and thinking of feeling! He chuckles and gets back to life. The screen is lit now with the word *ditz*.

This morning the guy from the insurance company shows up again in his nifty clothes. At his last meeting with Fred, he made a great effort to convince Fred that the *unpredictability* of life (while trying not to say *death*, perhaps) demands some kind of safeguard against loss. Fred concluded the discussion by stressing that for a single guy like him, death was the ultimate end and a loss against which no scheme of compensation could benefit him in any way. But now the insurance agent is back with a more compelling argument to back his policy's sale. He tells Fred to consider complete disability following some mishap, which may strike anyone at any time in life. Would he like to beg on the street, or be confined to bed and have to be provided his most basic needs? By moving the matter from death to *hard life*, the guy breaks the seal of Fred's defenses. After thinking in silence for a few minutes, Fred nods and asks about the policy. The agent opens his file with a triumphant mien.

Sleep seems to have lost its way somewhere in the dark tunnel that has been lurking in the way of Fred's peace. He is shifting from one side of his bed to the other, having a diffuse awareness of it being sometime past midnight. The terms of his insurance policy are marching up and down the lanes of his memory, their thudding synchronous with his heartbeat. It is a wonderful policy as far as his life is concerned. By its clauses, he will get enough coverage for all his basic needs if he happens to become *totally disabled*, and unable to work for a living, anytime in the next twenty years. After that period of time, which the insurance guy called the *term*, the policy may be renewed, though at a higher annual premium.

But then Fred's mind is no longer occupied with the details of the insurance policy. It is possessed by the repetitive thoughts of his funeral. (The insurance policy is supposed to cover all the expenses.) The agent briefly told him about the amount of compensation for the funeral, an amount which would vary according to the method of his body's disposal: *burial, cremation*, or *cryonic suspension*.

Fred's thoughts are now plodding through the dark screen of death in the dark room of his mind in this moonless night. The dark screen before his eyes changes subtly with each word that represents a possible method of disposal after death. *Burial* fills him with claustrophobic disgust; *cremation* brings a rush of frightening redness to his view, accompanied by a creepy crawl up his spine; *cryonic suspension* numbs his body down to its bones. Other scenes of possible disposal make their way in the cruelly laid out sheet of darkness. Being left in the open will let cannibalistic creatures tear his body to pieces; the same end will be caused by a surgeon's instruments if he donates his body to a medical research institute; the insides of some colossal fish will dissolve his remains in its acidic fluids if he chooses to be thrown into the ocean after his death.

The clock keeps ticking and the darkness of the screen before his eyes deepens until all the scenes of disposal are engulfed by plain blackness. The words associated with death all appear at the same time on the black screen: *foolish, crazy, coward, ditz.* He notices the absence of *brave.* Even as he thinks about it, the word does not show up, as if lost somewhere in the dark tunnel. Strangely enough, it makes him chuckle before he closes his eyes to sleep.

When the Straw Leaves

Surely it wasn't dark there, although evening shadows had grown on the lake. The two visitors eyed the blue water of the lake from the adjacent hill, enjoying the pleasant calm of it, even though there certainly were some waves springing near the center and traveling to the margins.

"Wow!" the lady exclaimed, charmed by the scene.

"Look at the ripples." The man asked her to watch the vibrant rings down there.

"Yes," she smiled. "They're beautiful."

"Indeed," he concurred. "But there isn't the least wind." He looked at her with a slight frown.

"Huh!" She considered his question, still fixing her gaze downward.

After a brief silence he said, "Well, it really makes them more beautiful, doesn't it, honey?"

She looked at him and saw that he had a thoughtfully pleasant expression. Then it instantly changed to a deep frown. She followed his gaze down to the lake. Now something had appeared in it, close to the center. A man's head broke the surface of the water; a young man most probably, with soaked dark hair, an average body, and appearing to be out of breath. He was facing them, water reaching just below his chin. It wasn't bright enough to see his face clearly but, by his appearance and style, he seemed familiar. Maybe he was one of those fun-loving guys who resorted to the lake for a swim. As the two of them stood on the hill watching the guy in the water, he seemed to have seen them from where he was in the water. And this was confirmed when he lifted his arms and waved at them, immediately to sink in the water again.

"He wants us to join him, perhaps," the wife said.

"No way!" her husband exclaimed, shaking his head with a smile. They were about to move on when the young man surfaced again, almost exactly where he had appeared before. He appeared disoriented, darting about in the water, looking for something, perhaps. As he caught sight of them, he shook his head to remove the hair from his eyes and took an arm out of the water to wave at them.

They stood still, somewhat confused.

"He isn't drowning, honey, is he?" the wife asked incredulously. Her husband gazed sharply at the young man, narrowing his eyes.

"He seems to recognize us," he said. "He's not drowning, or he would have shouted for help." He looked at his wife, who nodded in agreement, watching the man playing in the water—hands up, hands down, and so on again and again.

The husband waved his arms to him, with a loud "Enjoy!" The young man saw it and stopped beating the water. Obviously he wasn't happy with the idea of them leaving. Then he sank again.

They looked at each other and the lady said, "Honey, I'm afraid we aren't leaving any time for fun here."

"Yes," her husband approved, "let's go." And they started descending the hill. After a few steps down, suddenly the man stopped hesitantly.

"Honey, what is it?" the lady asked with some surprise. He looked at her in indecision and said, "Shouldn't we check one more time?" With this he took some steps back again.

She followed him to the top and stood beside him, watching the lake. He was still there, the guy in the lake. Now he wasn't facing them, rather they could see his back. He was still playing in the water, or struggling perhaps. The guy was looking at the bank on their side of the lake. Her gaze followed his and she saw the rather blurred silhouette of white color close to the shoreline. Clothes. Those were surely his clothes.

The man sighed, looked at his wife, and shrugged. She pouted, raising her brows, and then she smiled. He looked at the clothes once more, then at her, and smiled in return.

"Let's go, honey. It's getting late," she said, putting her arm around his waist.

"Yes." He did the same, and they turned to descend again. Stars had appeared in the sky. The moon was growing brighter.

They were long gone, and the figure in the water was no longer there. The lake was quiet and glossy, with no ripples. On the rocky shore, the clothes still lay to witness the calm of the night. All was quiet and peaceful except for the little evening moths that gathered around the clothes for the faint shine of light. It came from a small card with a silver stripe in its middle. It reflected the moonlight and the circles of moths danced around it, not capable of reading the carved capitals: APHONIC.

Ghosts

"Are you afraid of ghosts?" Kenneth Brand asked his wife, Jean, who worked as a fashion designer for an emerging company in Los Angeles.

"I don't believe in ghosts," answered Jean, faking an air of indifference. At thirty-six, she looked like a short, blond doll, with her hair bobbed about her neck. She was out with Kenneth for a walk in his hometown; they had stopped by his family's graveyard. It was getting dark, and she had already suggested that they return to his mother's house.

"So why would you not enter the graveyard?" Kenneth was looking to engage in some light-hearted reasoning.

"I don't know, but I think we should go back now." Jean was starting to feel a sense of aversion to the place where they both stood.

Kenneth pointed to the yard's almost square geometry of graves. "But I do want to take a walk around between those rows—unless, of course, you're afraid of ghosts."

"Yes, you know how they scare the breath out of me!" she snapped back, knowing his habit of teasing. "And especially so because I don't believe they exist!" She was on the edge of irritability.

He held her hand frankly. "Let's go in," he said, "and see if they *really* don't exist."

She liked the touch of his hand. It was as soothing and strengthening as a cordial. She walked at his side, keeping close to him, between the rows of graves, most of them nearly identical.

"Did you feel anything?" he asked as they reached the end of the last row, still holding hands.

She thought for a few seconds, looking at the graves behind her. Then she nodded lightly.

"What?" He took her face in both his hands.

She covered his hands with hers. "Well, you couldn't possibly have brought all those people so close together at one time in peace while they were still living."

He smiled in admiration.

"So where are the ghosts?" he asked.

They started to walk back along the grassy path, bypassing the geometry of graves.

"Hmm...I believe they're on their way to a family dinner." She clasped his arm in hers.

"And you still think we should go back to L.A. on Tuesday?" Kenneth's voice told her that he had already guessed her answer.

"Let's extend our time here another week."

She had told him what he wanted to hear, and what she really believed.

One Year!

One year! That is what he thought he had heard them say "One year to live." And then?

He stifled a sob rising up his chest, waking the pain that had been numbed for a while by the nurse's injection. Reclined against the pillows on his bed in that private health center, Robert Bennet was going through a time that he had never imagined in his worst nightmares. The invasion of symptoms that had started suddenly a couple of months ago had now been diagnosed as a fatal form of cancer. He remembered the physician's impersonal tone upon uttering its name—mesothelioma. Robert heard little after the doctor sorrowfully disclosed the fatal nature of his illness. The tests had confirmed it, and there was no cure—though he was free to believe in miracles, which he did not. Then the doctor's explanation fell on his deaf ears.

His hearing did, however, pick up the part where the maximum time of his future life was mentioned: one year. This hurt more than the shock of his terminal diagnosis. He didn't know why, but the indirect announcement of the estimated time of his death sounded more reckless than the disease that was about to cause it. *One year!* Next February, there would be no Robert Bennet breathing on this planet. No Robert Bennet! His heart sank within his chest. He wanted to cry, but was too lifeless for that now. Robert Bennet, dead at thirty-eight!

Beyond his control, the moment brought his struggle for success in life to mind. How he had pursued his long-desired career in architecture! From an insecure childhood to drudgery in mining, he had fought fatalism to see the bright days of success. And now, when he had arrived at his desired destination in an emerging construction firm, life had slapped him fatally in the face. He had stood firm against the dogma of fate, but now lay helpless as a feather in the path of fate's cruel march, inevitably to be trodden by it.

He moved his eyes to look about the room. Everything seemed so remote, as if he had nothing to do with the place and time in which these things existed and would continue to exist long after he was no more. He closed his eyes, breathing a painful sigh. In a year he'd be dead!

Suddenly it all felt like a joke. He felt uncontrollable laughter emerging like a series of short bubbles escaping through his dry mouth. A year of life! How funny! People would laugh if he told them so.

The thought of people suddenly filled his heart with deep-seated gloom. Who would mourn his death? Very few, if any, he thought. His parents were both dead, and so was the aunt he and his brother had lived with years ago. His brother Albert! Yes, he must go and see him. They met only once every couple of years or so. But then the thought of telling Albert about the doom awaiting him caused him yet more consternation. *What would it feel like?* No, he suddenly resolved, he must not tell Albert.

Let me die, and he won't have to worry about me this one whole year, he thought. But then the fear of loss loomed as he thought of dying without seeing his only kin. Albert lived far away from him, at nearly the opposite end of the country. Maybe it would be best to go and live with him before leaving him, and the world, for good.

Yes! Robert felt a spirited wave surging up his bosom, without invoking the pain. That would be the best thing, he thought, to go and spend whatever span of life he had left with his brother, his childhood friend. His insurance would cover the cost of his entire treatment, and he could sell his house and belongings to get enough money for several months. He had helped Albert so many times when he was in need. Now, he was sure, his brother would support him in these last days of his life.

Robert sat erect in his bed, feeling the blood moving through his veins, reminding him of the life he still had ahead him. Three hundred and sixty-five days, each one having twenty-four hours! The suppressed energy of his determination was rising against the diseased fate. He could surely do other good things while staying with Albert, like writing a few basic lessons on architecture for students; taking some nice photos, especially of the birds that he had always loved; cooking a few meals a week for Albert and himself; writing letters to the editors of local newspapers; going out with Albert, or a newly made friend, on a walk; and so many other things.

His spirits were getting up and about. One year of life was plenty. *A whole twelve months!* It was more than he would need to bring happiness and peace to his life and to that of others. He got off the bed, slipping his feet into his shoes. Yesterday was gone; tomorrow hadn't come yet; but he had today. It was time to start living life to the lees.

He picked up the roses on the table by his bedside and brought them closer to feel their beauty and aroma. Life had begun for Robert Bennet.

Tears for Blood

The bloody heel print was on the floor on one side of the wall, nowhere near the doorway. The rest of the shoe print was on the floor on the opposite side of the wall. It looked as if someone had walked there before the wall was set in place, but the house was old, the blood fresh. For a stranger it would have been a creepy scene. But Jo Raymond knew the whole story and so it was more somber than terrifying to see her father's blood still fresh and speaking for its innocence.

It was here, in this little cottage, that young Liam Raymond and his sweetheart Hannah had lived in unison of flesh and soul. Their life was bliss until the old craving for possessing Hannah turned her vicious cousin Morgan into a devil. In a stormy night when Liam was out to take Jo to her grandmother, Morgan broke in and tried to molest Hannah. She resisted and lost her life in the tussle. Before Morgan could escape, Liam returned. He was shocked to see the terrible disaster before him, and after a bloody combat with his foe, Morgan gutted him with a knife.

No one knew where Morgan fled to, but everyone knew that the last steps Liam had taken, with his feet covered in his blood, to reach his beloved wife's dead body couldn't be removed from the place. They appeared fresh after every effort to wash them away, or to scrape them off. Even when the walls of the cottage were readjusted, the blood stood wet and red as if it had been shed a minute ago. It didn't color the floor only but filled the color of revenge in Jo's life. She grew up with one single thought: *I must wash the blood of my father with that of her murderer.*

Her grandmother and her uncle had brought her up very well. She was beautiful, intelligent, and aggressively bold. Seeking a career in intelligence gathering, she set off to find Morgan Fields. Three years she hunted for him like a hungry hound. And one day when she got him, old Morgan, fifty-seven, lay paralyzed and blind in a nursing home, waiting for his death. That was what Jo had wanted to inflict on him, but she was stunned to see him. He couldn't speak or move. He couldn't hear but only stared into space like a dead statue. Jo did approach him and showed her Liam's photo. Nothing in him could respond but his eyes. They looked upon it and shed tears like rain, shivering and sobbing. And so the bottle she had taken with her to bring his blood was filled not with blood but tears, tears of compunction, of helplessness and suffering.

And now Jo Raymond was back again to wash the uneasy blood of her father, though she wasn't sure whether his soul would accept those colorless tears in place of the red blood like his own. Kneeling by the bloody print, Jo dropped the liquid on it and watched. It got dimmer and dimmer. The red color faded and disappeared. Tears welled up in her eyes. Her father's soul had gotten its peace. She rose slowly and walked to the other print to meet the last of her obligations.

The Choice

Dust could not cloud the road for Eric Smith the way his fuzzy thinking did at the moment. Driving his car to his Aunt Rebecca's house, Eric felt as if he were some mechanical contraption that had started to question the worth of its own function. He could hardly claim the expected confidence of a husband and a father toward his newborn infants. Confidence buttresses decisions. He had to make the choice in a finite amount of time. And he was anything but ready for it.

His wife and infants were left behind in the hospital, waiting their turn to secure a place in the desperate race of life. His nerves were throbbing. Would they make it? In the reckless game of survival, he had been given a chance to make a choice that might decide the survival of at least one member of his family. It was a trial he had never met before in his entire life. But now he had to face it while his courage failed him.

In a fit of panic, he could not think of anyone whom he could turn to except Aunt Becky, the nearest relative. She was the only one who lived close enough to weigh in on the emergency. As Eric's car raced toward her house, he felt his heart sinking.

* * * *

"Eric!" Rebecca's expression changed to a worried one the moment she opened the door and saw the pale, confused, anxious face of her nephew. "Is everything all right?" she asked, replacing part of the worry in her tone with a caring kindness. He sighed and looked at her, tears welling up in his eyes; then he could not hold them. The sight of her, the feeling of her presence, somehow felled his last bit of self-control.

"Oh, Eric!" She held his arm and led him inside. "What's the matter, my dear? Is Alicia all right? Tell me." Rebecca touched his cheek with her palm. He gave himself up to her embrace. There was no ground under his feet; he stood on the sense of her presence.

"Sit down my child, here!" As he sat in the chair, she poured him a glass of water, then stroked his hair gently as he gulped it.

"Tell me, now." She was anxious, but fought to keep from showing it, lest it weaken his budding control. "Tell me about it." He heaved out a deep, long-held sigh, somewhat recovered from the dreadful fear that had possessed him.

"The babies are born," he told her, fixing his gaze on the table.

"Are they all right?" Rebecca's voice was soft, soothing to his heart.

"No." He shook his head, pressing his lips together. "They are in a troubled situation, very much troubled."

"Tell me how," she said, and then remembered to add, "but first tell me if Alicia is okay."

"No. She's also unconscious, and the doctors say she's not safe yet. It was a terrible birth, something the hospital staff had never seen before." He was still shivering slightly.

"Eric!" Rebecca put her hand affectionately over his as she took a seat by his side. "I'm sure we do have reason to worry. But what about the babies?"

"They were born painfully the final hour and a half of labor. Alicia could not hold out and surgery was performed. The children were born alive, but now..." His voice yielded to a surge of his inner fear.

"Is there any hope for them?" Rebecca kept the softness of her voice. He looked at her with bleary eyes.

"Yes, but not both!" A sob left him.

"What!" Rebecca's look changed, and with a sigh, she pressed both his hands. "Tell me what's wrong."

"I haven't seen them." He freed his hand gently to wipe the corners of his mouth as he started to talk. "I didn't have the heart to see them. But the gynecologist told me that the heads of the babies were connected deep enough to reach their brains. They are experiencing some kind of seizures. The babies have been put on life support and they are in abnormal sleep. The doctors think that one of them has to..." He paused and then spoke with effort. "One of them has to die in order to let the other live. I've been asked to decide which one I would like to have live, the boy or the girl. I must tell them soon, or both..."

He hid his face in his hands and sobbed. His aunt got up and bent over to embrace him, kissing him on his head.

"It's a very difficult time, Eric," she whispered. "I'm sorry to hear it. But you are burdened with saving a life, and that you must do."

"Which one?" He raised his tearful eyes to her. "They are both my children, both my blood. How can I choose? *How?*"

"Whatever you decide will be the best, since they belong to you and you must save one of them. That is the best you can do." She ran her fingers through his disheveled hair.

"Alicia and I were so happy," he spoke feebly. "We never thought of any such trial. And it happened so suddenly. She's fighting for her life, and one of my children must die. I don't know what to do."

"What would you do if they were both girls, or both boys?" Rebecca suddenly posed a question, maintaining the calm of her voice.

"Maybe it would be different, easier, if they were both boys or both girls. But look at me. Where do I stand? Help me, Aunt Becky! Please help me out of this!" he entreated, and embraced her. She patted his back.

"I feel your anguish, Eric." She slowly moved away. 'But I cannot, and will not, decide for you. It's your blood, and you must make your choice. We are short of time for this, my dear child. I can't speak for you, though I can tell you about a memory that may give you the strength to make your choice."

"What memory?" He looked at her with strained eyes. She heaved a sigh, looked at him, and then turned away from him, taking a few steps.

'It's about Martha, your mother. There is something she never told you, right up to her death nine years ago."

"Mom?" Eric stood up from the chair and waited for her to speak.

"Yes." She turned to face him.

"Before she married your father, Martha married a reckless man she fell in love with while she was barely nineteen. Martha left with Jonathan to live with him at his family farmhouse. Our parents resented her marriage, and actually ordered her never to return.

"A year later, Martha's first child was born dead, a premature baby girl. Despite Dad's disapproval, Mom and I went to see Martha at the farmhouse. Grief had crushed her so recklessly. Jonathan was indifferent, rather than kind; later, we learned that he had been expecting a son. It was a disastrous time for my sister. But worse was yet to come."

Rebecca stepped toward the window, staring outside as if lost in some remote image. Then she spoke again, locking her arms tightly across her chest.

"It was two years later when she became pregnant again. Dad's anger had diminished a little, and we were allowed to visit Martha. She was a divided person then: half hope, half dread. The latter took over her life in the form of a living nightmare. Another stillborn daughter! Martha lived on only in name. She was dead in every true sense of the word.

"One evening, while Dad was still out, Jonathan left Martha at our home. He never returned to see her. How Mom and I managed to bring her back to life is a story too long to tell now, but somehow we pulled it off. Five years later, she was back in life, but this time with a dread that would never let go of her. We were happy to see Harry come into her life, giving her back her long-lost smiles. They got married, and despite their agreement not to have a child, Martha found herself pregnant.

"She started to have nightmares and panic attacks; her buried fears had surfaced. Harry said he was willing to let her have an abortion, because he wasn't sure that either one of them could stand the trial of the birthing process.

"I went to see her one evening, to see if she'd like to use abortion as the safer option. Martha looked at me as if transfixed, and then said that she would not kill the baby. She said, "This baby has a claim to life. I will never forgive myself if I let my fear prey on it." Then I knew how brave my sister was despite all her frailty.

"I was in the room, holding Martha's hand, while she gave birth to you. The hope of giving birth to life had beaten all her fears. I saw her smiling instead of showing the pain of birth. When you entered this life, it was the last day of my sister's fears. She chose to give you a chance, as it was more important to her than her apprehension of future or past fears."

Rebecca turned back to look at Eric. His eyes had spilled a rill of tears. She came close and took his face in her hands.

"Now it's your turn to decide in favor of the life of one of your children, without giving fear a chance to defeat you." They embraced each other as Eric's sobs gave way to a budding confidence.

Rebecca wiped his face with her fingers. "Go to the hospital now, and return with good news." She patted his cheek. He kissed her hand, nodded in acknowledgement, and left without saying a word.

* * * *

As Eric entered the obstetrics section of the hospital, Dr. Grace was coming out of Alicia's room.

"Eric!" She rushed to him. "It's good you're back.'

"How is she doing?" Eric asked impatiently.

"I'm glad to tell you that she's coming back to life." Dr. Grace gave him a brief, encouraging smile.

"She'll be okay?" Eric wanted more assurance.

"I think she'll be much better by tomorrow, maybe able to speak a few words. She's out of danger, we're sure of that," the doctor said. "But it's time now that we decide about the children, or else we'll be risking both infants. I know it's hard, Eric, but I must have your decision right away."

"I've decided," Eric spoke, fighting with the fear that was poking at his confidence from within. "I want..." He hesitated. Dr. Grace put her hand kindly on his shoulder, and he went on. "We are going to give the baby girl a chance."

About the Author

Karim Khan, pen named Ernest Dempsey, hails from Hangu, a small town in Pakistan. As a child, he enjoyed two things: The joyful company of his brother and Khan's best friend, Shais; and making airy castles with lots of characters in his mind. At twelve, he started writing detective stories, horror, thrillers, and humor. He has a Masters degree in Geology and one in English Literature.

He has authored four books and, in just the last few years, seen the publication of his poems, essays, short stories, and literary reviews worldwide. He is now the editor-in-chief of the literary magazine *Recovering the Self: A Journal of Hope and Healing* (www.RecoveringSelf.com) and also works as the country editor for Pakistan on the celebrated Internet news channel *Instablogs* (www.instablogs.com). Khan is now looking forward to completing his first novel. More about Khan and his works is available online at www.ErnestDempsey.com.

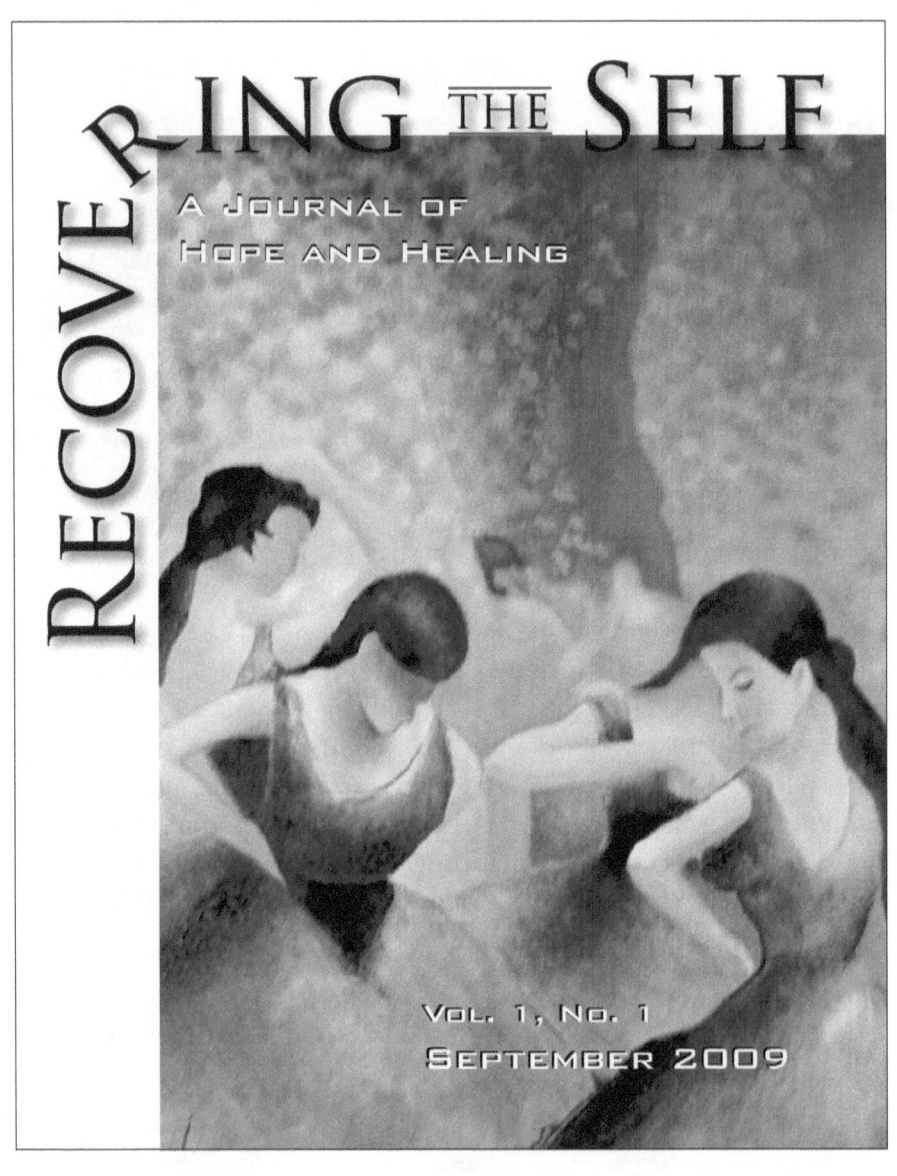

RECOVERING THE SELF

A JOURNAL OF HOPE AND HEALING

VOL. 1, NO. 1

SEPTEMBER 2009

EDITED BY ERNEST DEMPSEY

www.RecoveringSelf.com

www.ingramcontent.com/pod-product-compliance
Lightning Source LLC
Chambersburg PA
CBHW050310260626
47156CB00005B/1736